Music in My Heart

My Journey with Melody

by Erin Falligant
with Denise Lewis Patrick

✪ American Girl®

Published by American Girl Publishing

16 17 18 19 20 21 LEO 10 9 8 7 6 5 4 3 2 1

All American Girl marks, BeForever™, Melody™,
and Melody Ellison™ are trademarks of American Girl.

This book is a work of fiction. Any similarity to real persons, living or dead,
is coincidental and not intended by American Girl. References to real events,
people, or places are used fictitiously. Other names, characters, places, and
incidents are the products of imagination.

Grateful acknowledgment is made to the Rosa and Raymond Parks Institute
for Self Development for permission to reference Mrs. Parks.

Cover image by Michael Dwornik and Juliana Kolesova
Erin Falligant photo by Reverie Photography
Denise Lewis Patrick photo by Fran Baltzer Photo

americangirl.com/service

*For Mark, who understands
the power of music*

Beforever™

The adventurous characters you'll meet in
the BeForever books will spark your curiosity
about the past, inspire you to find your voice
in the present, and excite you about your future.
You'll make friends with these girls as you share
their fun and their challenges. Like you, they are
bright and brave, imaginative and energetic,
creative and kind. Just as you are, they are
discovering what really matters: Helping others.
Being a true friend. Protecting the earth.
Standing up for what's right. Read their stories,
explore their worlds, join their adventures.
Your friendship with them will BeForever.

A Journey Begins

This book is about Melody, but it's also about a girl like you who travels back in time to Melody's world of 1964. You, the reader, get to decide what happens in the story. The choices you make will lead to different journeys and new discoveries.

When you reach a page in this book that asks you to make a decision, choose carefully. The decisions you make will lead to different endings. (Hint: Use a pencil to check off your choices. That way, you'll never read the same story twice.)

Want to try another ending? Go back to a choice point and find out what happens when you make different choices.

Before your journey ends, take a peek into the past, on page 166, to discover more about Melody's time.

When Melody's story takes place, the terms "Negro," "colored," and "black" were all used to describe Americans of African descent. You'll see all of those words used in this book.

Today, "Negro" and "colored" can be offensive because they are associated with racial inequality. "African American" is a more contemporary term, but it wasn't commonly used until the late 1980s.

It's funny how one song can change *everything*.
I'm sitting at the piano on Saturday afternoon,
playing my recital piece again. The *tick, tick, tick* of the
metronome keeps my fingers moving, but my mind
wanders. *One more piano recital*, I remind myself. *Then
on to guitar!* Our fifth-grade class will learn guitar at
school this fall. I can picture it now . . . my best friend,
Anika, and me jamming together. Bye-bye, classical
music. Hello, pop!

The metronome grows louder. Then I realize that
the sound is actually my piano teacher, clapping her
hands to get my attention. "Stop, stop, stop . . ."
Ms. Stricker scolds. She's frowning. Anika and I don't
call her "Ms. Strict" for nothing!

My hands drop to my lap. "Did I make a mistake?"

"No," she says. "You're playing the notes perfectly.
But there's no *passion* in the piece—your heart's not
in it."

She sounds like my dad, who is always telling
me to "find my passion." He's a politician, so he's
really passionate about helping people and making a
difference in our community. *But what's my passion?*
I wonder. I'm not so sure it's piano. Sometimes when

I read music, it flows straight from my eyes to my fingertips. It must skip my brain, because I can think about something else while I'm playing. *Maybe it skips my heart, too,* I think sadly.

"Sorry," I say to Ms. Stricker, trying not to stare at the mole above her left eyebrow. If I blur my eyes, it looks like a quarter note without the stem.

Ms. Stricker sighs. She checks the clock on top of the piano. "I think," she says, "it's time for a different song."

A different song? The recital is only two weeks away! As Ms. Stricker rummages around in her cabinet, I hum the melody of my new favorite song, "Lemonade Days." I can't hit the high notes like Zoey Gatz does in her music video, but Anika can. I wish Ms. Stricker would let me play *that* song!

Instead, she hands me an old, stained piece of music with dog-eared corners. The title is "Lift Every Voice and Sing." "Try this one," she says.

As my fingers find the notes, the music takes shape. It sounds like the gospel songs my grandma and I used to sing at her church. As I play the slow, soulful song, I feel a pang of sadness. Grammy died a

3

few months ago. I can almost hear her singing the first line: *"Lift every voice and sing, till earth and heaven ring."*

When I reach the second verse, something happens. That single voice in my head swells, joined by other voices. I glance up from the keys, expecting to see a room full of people. There's no one there.

I can't hear the metronome anymore. I don't hear the phone ring either. When Ms. Stricker says she'll be right back—that she has to take a call—I keep playing. It's as if I can't stop.

"Let us march on till victory is won," the imaginary choir sings. And my fingers march on, too, across the keys. My heart speeds up, urging me toward the end of the song.

As I play the final note, I feel a breeze. The sheet music flutters, and the room darkens, as if someone pulled a curtain. I see nothing except the blue numbers on the digital clock, blinking 1:26, 1:26, 1:26. Then it all fades away.

♪ Turn to page 4.

I rub my eyes. The sheet music is still in front of me, but everything else has changed. There's a clock on the piano, but it's round and squat, with two bells on top. And this isn't Ms. Stricker's piano at all! Hers is made of shiny mahogany, almost red. This piano is lighter and covered with a fine layer of dust.

There's a bulletin board hanging above the piano. My eyes are drawn to a familiar face—a black man—staring out from a poster. "Walk to Freedom with Dr. Martin Luther King Jr.," the poster reads. I squint to read the print at the bottom: "Detroit, Michigan. Sunday, June 23, 1963."

"Wow!" says a girl's voice from behind me.

I whirl around. She's standing in the doorway: a girl about my age wearing a sleeveless green-and-blue-checked dress that pops against her golden brown skin. The dress is short and flares out at the hem. It reminds me of the dress my grandma is wearing in a photo of her as a teenager.

"That was *amazing*," the girl says.

What is she talking about? I wonder, turning back to the poster. "The, um, Walk to Freedom, you mean?" I stammer.

She laughs. "No, silly—your piano playing!" she says. "But the Walk to Freedom here in Detroit last summer was pretty amazing, too. My family and I marched in it."

Last summer? The poster says that the Walk to Freedom happened in June of 1963. I do the math. That was more than fifty years ago.

Then I notice the room around me. It's filled with fold-up tables and chairs, like a meeting hall. On the table closest to me, I see an old typewriter. My mom has one in her office, but just for decoration. It's too hard to press down on those raised keys. There's a black telephone on the table, too, with a long, twisted cord. My grandma had one like that in her apartment.

Everything in this room seems old-fashioned, like a scene from a black-and-white movie. A question swirls through my mind. *Is this my craziest daydream ever, or did I just play my way back in time?*

🎵 *Turn to page 6.*

I 'm Melody," says the girl in the doorway, "and I *love* the song you just played. So does my grandma. She's here at church, upstairs. If I go get her, will you play it again?"

Her brown eyes smile at me from beneath her turquoise headband. She's real. This can't be a daydream!

"Please?" she asks.

When I nod, the girl spins on her heel. I hear her footsteps clattering up a set of stairs.

I try to remember the last time anyone seemed so happy to hear me play piano. Definitely not Ms. Strict at lessons this afternoon! But there *is* something special about the song I just finished. My fingers stroke the keys again, softly at first. But after the first verse, I barely need to read the music. I sail through it, hearing the voices rise up around me.

> *Sing a song full of the faith*
> *that the dark past has taught us,*
> *Sing a song full of the hope*
> *that the present has brought us.*

I close my eyes and let the music fill me up. As the

last notes fade away, I hear a *tick, tick, tick.* I open my eyes and see the silver bar of Ms. Stricker's metronome. It swings from side to side, as if gesturing toward the clock on the piano—the clock with blue numbers that still read 1:26.

When Ms. Stricker steps into the room, I jump. Then I see the expression on her face. She's actually smiling.

"That was beautiful," she says—for the first time ever. I've heard her say "perfect," but never "beautiful."

Pride swells in my chest, followed by excitement. I did it again! I played this magical song and somehow traveled through time. Then I think of Melody, that mysterious girl I left behind. My fingers itch to play the song again and get back to her in that basement room.

"Your mom will be here in a couple of minutes," Ms. Stricker says. "Take the music home with you, my dear. Polish it up and make it yours."

I place the music carefully in my book bag. This song already feels like mine, more than anything else I've ever played. *Wait for me, Melody,* I think, trying to send a message across time. *I'll be back soon!*

🎵 *Turn to page 8.*

"id you hear me, honey?" Mom asks from the driver's seat on the way home.

"Huh?"

"Wow, you're really in la-la land," she says, patting my knee.

More like Melody land, I want to say.

"I said I have some bad news," Mom says, growing serious. "Budgets are tight this year, and that's going to mean changes at school this fall."

Mom is the principal of my school, which has its pluses and minuses. Some kids think I get special treatment. But mostly, I just get to hear news about the school before other kids do.

"The music program may have to scale back," Mom says slowly.

That gets my attention. "What do you mean?" I ask, sitting up. My seat belt squeezes against my chest.

Mom sighs. "There aren't enough instruments for all the students, and there's no money to buy more. So there may not be any guitars this year, sweetie."

She might as well have socked me in the stomach. I can't breathe.

"I'm still working on it," she says, "but . . ."

"But it's already August!" I blurt. "School starts in less than a month!"

"I know, honey," says Mom. "It doesn't look good."

We drive on in silence, and then she says, "Dad is campaigning this afternoon, so it's just you and me."

Again? I think. Dad has been working hard to get reelected to Congress. He stays up late writing speeches, and he's gone a lot at night and on the weekends. *Dad has plenty of passion for his job,* I think. *Ms. Strict would approve.*

"Want to join me in my office for a while?" Mom asks as we turn into our driveway.

She has a special corner in her home office with a purple beanbag chair and fuzzy blanket. I curl up there sometimes and read while Mom is working. But today, I want to go straight to my room. I'm bummed about the guitars, but I know what will make me feel better: I have to find my way back to Melody. Will she still be there?

"I . . . um . . . want to practice more," I say, holding up my folder with piano music inside.

"Really?" says Mom, raising her eyebrows.

I can't blame her. I'm usually not much for

practicing. "I have a new song," I quickly explain. "For the recital in two weeks."

I burst through the front door ahead of Mom and try my hardest not to run across the living room. If I race to practice the piano, Mom will *really* know something's up! Instead, I walk slowly down the hall, running my fingertips along the spines of the books on the shelves.

My family must own every book ever printed, and we all love to read. My mom reminds me of how lucky we are. She says lots of kids don't have books of their own—even the ones they need to do their schoolwork.

I would grab a book right now, but there's something else I need to do. I close my bedroom door behind me and hurry to the keyboard beneath my window. Anika's photo, in a heart-shaped frame on the window ledge, catches my eye. Her knowing eyes bore into me from beneath her black bangs, as if to say, "I know you have a new secret. Tell me. Please!"

I tell Anika *everything*, even the stuff that's kind of impossible to believe, like meeting Melody. I fish my phone out of my pocket and send her a quick text: *You won't believe what happened today.*

Then I lean toward the window, straining to see if Anika's mom is working in the flower beds two houses down. Anika's yard is empty, but the new girl is playing in the yard next door. She's throwing a Frisbee to her little brother, calling something to him in Spanish.

When she glances my way, I duck, almost hitting my chin on my keyboard. Did she see me? I don't want her to think I'm spying on her.

I settle back in front of my keyboard and turn it on. Do I need to play a piano to get back to Melody or will this work? I start to pull the sheet music out of my bag, but I stop mid-reach. I don't need the music anymore— I know I don't. I feel as if I've been playing this song my whole life.

I take a deep breath, close my eyes, and begin again.

🎵 *Turn to page 12.*

e're back!"

Melody's voice sends a joyful tingle down my spine. I'm at the piano in the church basement again. *It worked!* I think. *As long as I play "Lift Every Voice and Sing," I can get to Melody and back home again.*

When I turn to smile at Melody, I see an older woman standing in the doorway with her. She's not much taller than Melody, and she's flicking a paper fan in front of her face.

"This is Big Momma—oops, I mean Mrs. Porter," Melody says. "She's my grandma."

"Mmm, mmm," Mrs. Porter says, shaking her head. "I don't know what's warming me up more—this August heat, or that glorious song you just played, child."

She liked my playing! Her smile warms me up, too, from the inside out. "Thank you, ma'am . . . um, Mrs. Porter."

"Where'd you learn to play like that?" Melody asks, skipping over to the piano bench. She smells like fresh air and flowers.

"Piano lessons," I admit. "Lots of lessons." *Too many,* I used to think. But right now, I'm proud of what I've

learned to do. My cheeks are burning.

"You're really good," says Melody. "Are you part of the traveling youth choir that's visiting our church?"

"Mercy me," says Mrs. Porter, overhearing. "I think that choir bus is leaving soon. Did you get lost in the music, baby? We'd better get you upstairs." She waves me toward the door.

Melody sees me hesitate. She tilts her head and asks, "Or are you here for the Student Walk to Freedom Club? My big sister, Yvonne, is leading that. We drove her here. She'll be down any minute."

🎵 *To follow Mrs. Porter upstairs,*
turn to page 17.

🎵 *To wait here and meet Melody's sister,*
turn to page 14.

I don't want Mrs. Porter to put me on a bus. I just got here! And if Melody's sister Yvonne is anything like Melody, I want to meet her.

Clearing my throat, I say, "I'm not with the choir. I'd, um, like to stay for the meeting."

"The Student Walk to Freedom Club?" Melody repeats. "Good. Maybe I can stay, too." She looks at her grandma with pleading eyes.

"That's all right by me," says Mrs. Porter. "But you girls will have to walk home after."

Melody nods. "Thanks, Big Momma."

After she leaves, teenagers begin to file into the room. Melody keeps her eye on the door. Finally, she points. "There's Yvonne!" A pretty young woman rushes in wearing an orange blouse and a patterned scarf over her head. There's a cast on her left wrist.

"Hey, Dee-Dee," she says to Melody. "I didn't expect you here." Then she gets pulled away by another young woman who is gesturing toward the clock.

Yvonne steps to the front of the room. "Thank you for joining us this week," she says. "Thank you for coming from other churches and towns to help the Student Walk to Freedom Club. Some of us are just

back from the Mississippi Summer Project, and we've got a lot to tell you. Together, we're making a *difference* for black people all over the country!"

As people whistle and cheer, I scoot closer to Melody. "What's the Mississippi Summer Project?" I whisper.

She leans over and says, "A bunch of college students—black and white—went to Mississippi. They helped black people register to vote, and they set up Freedom Schools for black kids. Yvonne says voting is really important."

I nod. "My dad says that, too," I whisper. "He's a politician, and he's always saying how important it is to get out and vote."

"Wow," says Melody. "Your dad is a politician?"

The way she looks at me makes me feel proud. I hope she doesn't ask what my dad does, though, because I'm not exactly sure. He's gone a lot. He travels to Washington, D.C., but I don't really know what he does there. I don't ever ask him, because politics seems like grown-up stuff.

I have trouble paying attention to Yvonne's speech, because I'm busy looking around the room. It's full

of young people. Most of them are older than me and Melody, but they're still younger than the people who show up for my dad's speeches.

All of a sudden Yvonne looks right at me and Melody and says, "There's plenty we can do to help black people right here in Detroit. And that's where *you* come in."

Me? I think, slinking down in my seat. *What can girls like Melody and me do?*

I glance at Melody. She's leaning forward, like she's ready to get started *now.*

♪ *Turn to page 20.*

(u)m, I did get a little lost in the music," I admit, because it's true.

Mrs. Porter clucks her tongue, but her eyes are smiling. "Well then, girls," she says. "Follow me."

As we cross the room, Melody sings softly. *"Lift every voice and sing, till earth and heaven ring."* Her voice is pure and sweet, like Anika's.

"You're a really good singer!" I say.

Melody flashes a smile. "Thanks. We sang that song for Youth Day last fall." She lowers her voice shyly and adds, "I had a solo."

I'm not surprised to hear that. If I had a voice like Melody's, I'd be brave enough to sing all by myself. But I could never sing alone in front of a crowd.

Mrs. Porter waves us along. When she puts her hand on my shoulder, I smell flowers again. Big Momma smells like roses.

When we reach the bend in the stairs, we run into a woman wearing a tidy suit and high heels. "Miss Dorothy!" says Melody. "This is our choir director," she explains to me.

"Just the woman we're looking for," Mrs. Porter says. "Is the youth choir getting ready to leave?

We found one of its members playing her sweet heart out downstairs."

Miss Dorothy stares at me through little round glasses. "Oh, dear," she says. "That bus left fifteen minutes ago."

Melody sucks in her breath.

"The choir is heading north for a few shows before coming back for their Tuesday night performance," Miss Dorothy says. "I wonder if someone can drive her to catch the bus . . ." She checks her watch.

"It's all right," I say quickly. "I can get myself back home." I don't want to catch that bus, not knowing where it's going. And besides, why would I want to leave Melody and Mrs. Porter right now, when I'm just getting to know them?

Melody's eyes sparkle like fireworks. "If the traveling choir is coming back Tuesday," she says thoughtfully, "maybe someone from the congregation could let her stay with them till then. Maybe *you* could take her in, Big Momma. Couldn't you?"

Mrs. Porter hesitates, and then her face eases into a smile. "Don't fret, Melody," she says. "We wouldn't turn this little chick away now, would we?"

I smile right back—I can't help it. There's something so comforting about Melody's grandma. When Melody wraps her arms around her, I want to hug her, too.

Melody grabs my hand. "Oh, we're gonna have so much fun!"

I can already feel it—that tingle running from my fingertips to my toes, telling me that I'm about to set off on an amazing adventure.

"Now, I suspect your suitcase is riding on that bus you missed," says Mrs. Porter.

Suitcase? I didn't think about that. I glance down at what I'm wearing. This is all I have with me!

"That's okay," says Melody brightly. "You can borrow some clothes from me. We're about the same size." She seems pretty happy that I'm staying, and I am, too.

As I follow her out of the church and into the sunshine, I remind myself that I can go home anytime I want. I just have to play that song and I'll be back in my bedroom—as if no time has passed at all.

I smile, skipping down the steps after Melody.

🎵 *Turn to page 22.*

*Y*vonne tells us exactly what we can do to help: stuff envelopes, make posters, and help cook food for volunteers. Those all sound like things I can do—except for maybe the cooking part.

Then Yvonne picks up a clipboard. "Let's talk about where you'll be staying this week," she says. "Those of you from out of town have been paired up with host families from our church." She taps the clipboard. "Has anyone not met their family yet?"

Uh-oh. I'm not on that list! Where will I stay?

Melody is way ahead of me. "You can stay with me," she says. "Or . . . do you have another place?"

I shake my head. "I didn't plan on staying. I just wanted to hear what the meeting was all about, but . . . I'd like to stay—at least for a couple of days."

Melody smiles, her eyes bright. "I'll call Mommy," she says. She uses the black telephone on the card table, lifting the phone to her ear and using her finger to spin a round wheel on the base of the phone.

When she hangs up, I can tell by the grin on her face that her mom said yes. "Do you have to call home, too?" she asks.

I hesitate. Back home, Mom is still working in her

office. She isn't missing me. And even if she were,
I can't call her from an old phone in 1964. Mom wasn't
even born back then!

🎵 *Turn to page 25.*

Have you been to Detroit before?" Mrs. Porter
asks. She's looking at me in her rearview mirror
as we drive away from the church.

"What? No, never, ma'am," I say. I'm only half listening, because I just realized there are no seat belts in
the back of the car! Melody isn't even searching for one.
So I settle back in my seat, too, and try not to worry.

Luckily, Mrs. Porter is a careful driver. As she pulls
up to a stoplight, the nose of her car stretches out long
in front of us. *All* of the cars around us are long, low,
and narrow. I'm used to being up higher when I ride in
my mom's SUV.

"You'll be seeing all kinds of new places with the
traveling choir, won't you?" Mrs. Porter continues. "You
know, it seems like a hundred years ago now, but I was
once in a traveling singing group, too."

"With Miss Dorothy," Melody pipes up. "They had
their own gospel group."

Mrs. Porter winks at me in the mirror. "In fact," she
says, "Miss Dorothy and I are going to go hear some
gospel music downtown after dinner. It's a special
show—the owners of the performance hall are friends
of mine from way, way back."

"Do you mean Auntie Josephine and Uncle Al?" asks Melody. "Oh, I wish we could go, too."

Mrs. Porter has a twinkle in her eye when she says, "Well, maybe you can—if your momma says it's all right." When the light in front of us turns green, she eases the car forward.

"You'll love the performance hall," Melody says to me in a breathy voice. "There's a big stage and a piano. They have lots of parties there, and recitals. My youth choir was even onstage once! And they have concerts with *amazing* gospel music. I'm not sure what's more fun—singing there or listening to someone else perform."

"It sounds awesome," I say. I've only heard gospel music at church, and on my grandma's old records. I'm excited to go to a concert with Melody, but somehow, sadness creeps into my chest again as I think about Grammy.

As soon as we reach Mrs. Porter's, though, I feel better. The first thing I see in her living room is an old upright piano. It's taller than Ms. Stricker's, and there are flowers carved into the music stand. It's beautiful! My fingers itch to play. Would Mrs. Porter mind?

She's already nudging me with her hand. "Go on," she says with a chuckle. "Play me something pretty while I work in the kitchen."

🎵 *Turn to page 27.*

t's okay," I tell Melody. "My parents want me to get involved in things like this."

It's true. My dad would be excited to know that I'm learning about helping people vote. And Mom is all about kids getting a good education. Maybe I can ask her if she knows about the Mississippi Summer Project when I get home.

After the meeting, Melody and I walk to her house. It's a sticky August afternoon, but the walk gives us time to talk.

As we pass a pretty park, Melody pauses by the fence. "My friends and I just fixed this up," she says. "We started a Junior Block Club this spring, and we painted those benches and planted all these flowers. We're even growing vegetables."

"Really?" I say. "You and your friends did all that by yourselves?" Anika and I tried to build a tree house in our neighborhood once, but we gave up after half a day. It seemed like too much work for kids.

"Well, we had help from Miss Esther, who lives across the street," she says, nodding toward a yellow house. "And my grandpa helped us plant that vegetable garden."

A garden, too? Wow. Maybe that's why Melody didn't seem scared listening to Yvonne talk about how we could make a difference. Melody's already doing it!

Melody pushes open the gate, and I follow on her heels. We both hop on one foot down the hopscotch board painted on the sidewalk. And soon we're hanging upside down on the jungle gym.

As Melody sits up, she asks, "What grade are you going into this year?"

"Fifth," I say, feeling a bit dizzy as I sit up, too.

"I knew it!" she says. "So am I." She flashes me a smile.

And I already know something else, I think with a grin. *We're going to be great friends.*

When Melody leaps off the jungle gym and lands in the soft dirt below, I follow her, shrieking with laughter.

♪ *Turn to page 30.*

While Melody settles onto the sofa, I play a few scales. The piano keys are more yellow than white, but the sound is pure and rich—more *real* than the "tinny" sound of my electric keyboard.

"Play a song," says Melody.

My mind goes blank. I can't play "Lift Every Voice and Sing." That'll take me home! I start to play my recital piece, but Ms. Stricker was right—it sounds flat. So I play the song in the open music book in front of me: "We Shall Not Be Moved."

Mrs. Porter pops her head through the swinging door. "You know that one, too, baby?" she asks, wiping her hands on her apron.

"No," I admit. "This is my first time playing it."

Melody scoots to the edge of the couch. "You've *never* played it before?" she asks, sounding surprised. "You're really good at reading music."

Mrs. Porter shakes her head. "Have mercy," she says. "Go on and sing with her, Melody. The two of you have more talent between you than most congregations put together."

As I start to play again, Melody's voice blends with the rich notes of the piano.

We shall not,
We shall not be moved.
We shall not,
We shall not be moved.
Just like a tree that's standing by the water,
We shall not be—

Just then, the front door opens, and a tall teenager bursts into the room.

"Aha!" he says. "I thought I heard the voice of my favorite sister, the extraordinary Melody Ellison."

She laughs and runs to hug him. "What're you doing here, Dwayne?"

"And did you forget how to knock?" scolds Mrs. Porter.

"Big Momma, I knocked," says Dwayne. "You just didn't hear me over the choir." He winks at Melody and then notices me. "Don't stop playing on my account," he says. "I'll join you."

As he sits down beside me on the bench, I suddenly feel shy. I have to wipe my sweaty palms on my pants. When Melody stands beside me, though, I feel better— especially when she starts to sing.

Then Dwayne taps out the rhythm with his hand on the side of the piano. And Mrs. Porter begins clapping her hands on the offbeat. Pretty soon, I hear her deep voice layered beneath Melody's sweet, high voice.

Dwayne sings softly, too. *"We're fighting for our freedom, we shall not be moved,"* he croons.

The music fills me up and spills over, like a wave of happiness. *Is this what Ms. Stricker meant by playing with passion?* I wonder. I don't want the song to ever end.

Then, as I play the last few notes, something happens: Melody keeps singing. Is there another verse?

I turn the page, but that's it—it's the end of the song. What should I do? I don't want to mess up!

🎵 *Turn to page 31.*

(w) hen we get to Melody's house, no one's home—except for her dog, Bo. I scratch the black-and-white terrier behind the ears, and he wags his tail.

"C'mon," says Melody, racing toward the stairs with the dog at her heels. "I'll show you my bedroom."

Her room is small, but it holds three beds. "I share this with my sister Lila," says Melody. "Vonnie moved across the hall to Dwayne's old room, so you can sleep in her old bed."

"You have another sister?" I ask, trying to imagine three girls fitting in here with all their stuff.

"Yeah," says Melody. She sits down on a bed with a bright orange bedspread. "Lila's fourteen and she'll be starting at a private school this fall. She and my mom are out buying her textbooks right now. My brother, Dwayne, calls Lila 'Miss Bookworm' because she's *always* reading."

Melody has a brother, too? She's got such a big family! I can't wait to meet them all. Then I notice a stack of books by her bed. There's one by Langston Hughes and a worn copy of *The Secret Garden*.

🎵 *Turn to page 34.*

(m) elody keeps singing, even though I've stopped
playing. Her grandmother and brother do, too.

"Just like a tree . . ." Mrs. Porter sings, swaying her
shoulders as she claps.

"Ooh, ooh, ooh," adds Dwayne.

So I put my hands on the keys and repeat the last
few bars of the song. I don't know what else to do! It
seems to work, the notes and the voices around me
blending into one.

Then somehow, magically, we all stop at the exact
same moment. The hairs stand up on my arms. For a
few seconds, there's pure silence.

"Whoo!" says Dwayne. "That was some jam."

I laugh with relief. "I thought I was going to mess
up," I admit.

"Really?" says Melody. "You were so good!"

"And remember," says Mrs. Porter. "There's no
messing up with improvisation."

"That's right. Lots of Motown artists improvise,"
Dwayne adds. "They make up their own words or
melodies while they play."

"Motown?" I ask, wanting to understand.

Dwayne's jaw drops open. "Girl, have you been

living under a rock?" he asks. "Motown is Mr. Berry
Gordy's record label here in Detroit. He puts out
music by The Temptations, The Supremes, Little Stevie
Wonder . . ."

I recognize that last name, sort of. I nod with relief.

"It's not just musicians who improvise," Mrs. Porter
says. "Preachers do, too. Our own Dr. Martin Luther
King didn't just read the words of his 'I Have a Dream'
speech. Every time he gave the speech he changed it a
little bit, depending on the event and the audience. He
let his heart find the words as he spoke."

Mrs. Porter talks about Martin Luther King as if
she knows him. Then I remember that Melody and her
family heard him speak at the Detroit Walk to Freedom
last summer. I get chills, imagining what that must
have been like.

"You know," says Melody, "my brother's a Motown
star, too. His group, The Three Ravens, just recorded a
song!"

"Really?" I say. Suddenly, I can't look at Dwayne.
He's a real star—like Zoey Gatz.

"But that's not the whole story, Dee-Dee," he says.
"Are you gonna tell your friend that you're officially

a recording artist now, too?"

A slow smile spreads across Melody's face, and I can tell she's excited. "I recorded with Dwayne at the studio," she says. "Just singing backup, though."

My jaw drops. I can't believe I just jammed with not one Motown star, but two!

🎵 *Turn to page 37.*

I read that," I say, pointing toward *The Secret Garden*.

Melody follows my gaze. "It's one of my all-time favorite books," she says. "I *love* gardens. My grandpa says I got my green thumb from him. Poppa grew up on a farm in Alabama. We actually took a trip to see it last month."

"Was it fun?" I ask, sitting down on the bed. I used to love taking trips with my grammy.

Melody nods. "So much happened! We stayed with my mom's Aunt Beck, and we got to see lots of cousins on the Fourth of July. We talked about how great it is that President Johnson signed the Civil Rights Act. Now it's the law that black people have to be treated equally. My mom says it's what we've been protesting and marching for all this time." A shadow passes over her face as she adds, "But not everyone is happy about the new law. Some scary things happened, too."

"Like what?" I ask, scooting closer.

Melody pulls her knees to her chest. "Everyone was talking about the three civil rights workers who disappeared in June." She shivers. "They were part of the Mississippi Summer Project, like Yvonne, trying

to help black people register to vote. But white people complained and the police arrested them. They just vanished, and they're still missing." Melody's lip trembles. "While we were still in Alabama, we found out . . ." Melody takes a shaky breath. "We found out Yvonne was arrested, too."

I suck in my breath. "She went to *jail*?"

Melody nods. "That's how she broke her wrist. She tripped while the police were arresting her. Mommy and Poppa had to go get her out of jail the next day."

I don't even know what to say. Melody must have been afraid that her sister would disappear, too. I can't understand why anyone would try to keep black people from having equal rights.

I want to tell Melody that things are better now—in my time—but a memory tickles the back of my mind. My family had gone out to eat with Mr. Chapman, Dad's campaign manager, who is black. When Mr. Chapman stepped outside, a white man handed him his car keys.

I tell Melody that story.

"Why'd he do that—with the keys?" she asks.

"Because he thought Mr. Chapman was a *valet*,

someone who parks cars for customers eating at the restaurant. He thought that because Mr. Chapman was black, he must be working there, not out to dinner. Dad says things like that still happen a lot."

Melody shakes her head. "It's not fair," she says. "It's discrimination to treat someone differently just because of the color of their skin."

Bo whines from his spot on the rug, as if agreeing with her.

Then Melody hops up and says, "That's why Yvonne says we gotta *do* something. We have to make it better, even here in Detroit."

I smile. I like that Melody wants to help other people—that she's not afraid to try, even though she's young like me. And that makes me want to make things better, too.

🎵 *Turn to page 39.*

peaking of Motown, I've gotta run," says Dwayne, standing up and stretching his long legs. "We have a rehearsal at the studio tonight, and I've gotta take care of some things before then."

As he kisses Mrs. Porter's cheek, I try to think of something to say. Should I get his autograph? My mouth goes dry.

Before I can say anything, Dwayne is on his way out the door. But all of a sudden, he stops and turns around. "Hey, Dee-Dee, do you and your friend want to hang out at the studio tonight and watch the rehearsal?"

Yes! I think.

"Yes!" says Melody. "Wait, no—we're going to listen to gospel music with Big Momma tonight."

Melody looks just as torn about that as I feel. Going to the studio would be so cool! But we already told Mrs. Porter we'd go to the performance hall with her, and that'll be fun, too.

Mrs. Porter says, "Don't you chicks fret. You go on down to the studio if that's what you want to do." Her warm smile says she means it, but somehow, that doesn't make our decision any easier.

Melody looks at me with a question in her eyes:
What do we do?

♪ To go hear gospel music with Mrs. Porter,
turn to page 43.

♪ To visit Dwayne at the studio,
turn to page 46.

I get to see Yvonne again at dinner that night, along with Melody's sister Lila and their parents.

Melody's parents are kind of like mine. Her mom is a teacher, like Mom used to be before she became a principal. And Melody's dad, who works at a car factory, is gone a lot, just like mine.

But everything else about Melody's big family is way different. When she and her sisters start talking, the whole room fills with their voices and laughter. It's never *this* noisy at my house!

After dinner, I'm watching Lila braid Melody's hair in their bedroom. Yvonne, with a towel wrapped around her wet head, is curled up on the bed giving instructions.

Music pipes out of the radio on the headboard—"Motown music," Melody calls it. Her foot taps along to the beat.

"Melody, sit still!" Yvonne says, laughing. "You're making it hard for Lila."

"She sure is," says Lila, pushing her glasses up on her nose. "I'm getting better at it, though."

"You're still not quite as good as Yvonne is," says

Melody. "When is that wrist gonna heal again?"

Yvonne sighs. "Not soon enough."

I'm dying to ask her about her broken wrist—about how it happened and what it was like to be arrested. But that wouldn't be polite. Instead, I ask, "Does it hurt much?"

Yvonne shakes her head. "Not too much. And when it does? I just remind myself how it happened, and that makes me mad enough to forget the pain." She smiles, but I know she's being serious.

"You're so brave, Vonnie," says Melody. "I wish I were as brave as you."

Yvonne reaches out to grab her sister's toes. "You are, Dee-Dee. And anyway, I wish I were as good a *singer* as you."

Melody laughs and yanks her foot away.

"Sit still, Dee-Dee!" says Lila with an exasperated sigh. Then, after a moment of silence, she asks, "So don't either of you wish you were as s*mart* as me?"

That cracks me up. Melody laughs, too, which Lila doesn't seem to appreciate. "You're smart all right, Lila," she says, patting her sister's arm. "Big Momma says we've all got our own lights to shine."

At that, Melody catches Yvonne's eye. And then the sisters erupt into song. *"This little light of mine,"* sings Melody. *"I'm gonna let it shine."*

Hey, I know this song!

Yvonne sings into a hairbrush, as if it were a microphone. *"This little light of mine, I'm gonna let it shine."*

Lila finally gives up and lets go of Melody's hair. *"This little light of mine, I'm gonna let it shine,"* she adds in her high soprano voice.

And even I jump in for the last line: *"Let it shine, let it shine, let it shine."*

"Let's do it in rounds!" says Melody, standing up. When Bo jumps up on her legs, she takes his front paws and dances with him around the room.

"This little light of mine," she sings. And Bo adds two barks, right on beat.

We sing, laugh, and bark our way through a whole round, until someone raps loudly on the door. "What on earth is going on in here?" Melody's mom asks, poking her head into the room.

"Sorry, Mommy," says Melody, laughing. "Just doing our sister-thing." She looks at me. "That's what Dwayne calls it, anyway."

This sister-thing is so fun! I wish these girls were my sisters, too. Maybe I'm even a little like them. I like to read books, like Lila. I love music, like Melody. And I hope someday I'll be just as brave as Yvonne.

Later, I'm lying in Yvonne's old bed in Melody and Lila's room. I feel a pang of homesickness, like I always do at sleepovers. But then I hear Melody's daddy snoring down the hall. And is that Yvonne talking on the phone downstairs? I strain my ears. Then Bo starts scratching at his collar at the foot of Melody's bed: *jingle, jingle, jingle.*

The sounds blend together like music. *It was music that brought me here to meet Melody,* I remember. So it's no wonder that her house is so full of joyful sound.

This little light of mine, I hum, remembering the sister-thing. And then I'm not homesick anymore.

🎵 *Turn to page 45.*

think we should go listen to gospel music," I say. Maybe it's because Mrs. Porter reminds me of my grandma. There's no one I'd rather spend the evening with than my grandma—not even Zoey Gatz. I miss Grammy so much!

Melody nods. "Me, too," she says. "Sorry, Dwayne."

"Some other time," he says with an easy grin. Then he ducks out the door and is gone.

"Good, that's settled," Mrs. Porter says, her cheeks dimpling. "Now why don't you two come and have a snack while I make supper."

"Okay," says Melody, racing toward the kitchen. "C'mon!"

As we push through the swinging door, I glance around the tidy kitchen. The first thing I notice is the refrigerator. It's white and rounded, with one door instead of two. Doesn't it have a freezer?

As Mrs. Porter opens the door to get a pitcher of lemonade, I see the freezer—it has its own inside door. She opens it, slides out an ice cube tray, and pops a couple of cubes into each glass on the counter.

"Thank you, Mrs. Porter," I say as she places a glass in front of me.

She touches my cheek with the back of her hand and says, "Go ahead and call me 'Big Momma,' baby. "It's okay."

My heart melts like an ice cube on a hot August day. I want to hug her and never let go.

♪ *Turn to page 49.*

Sunday morning, I go to church with Melody's family. Mrs. Porter pats the bench, inviting me to slide in next to her. As we sing the first hymn, I remember the song that brought me here: "Lift Every Voice and Sing." Will I still be able to play the music when it's time to go home? My fingers begin to tap out the notes on my lap. *Yes*, I think, smiling. *How could I ever forget?*

After the service, Melody and I go down to the community room for another Student Walk to Freedom Club meeting. It's time to choose a project. "Some of us will stay here and make signs," Yvonne says. "We're picketing the Windwood grocery store this week because they won't hire black people."

A low murmur ripples through the room.

"If enough people show up, Windwood *has* to listen," Yvonne continues. "So we'll need plenty of signs for picketing."

"Making signs could be kind of fun," Melody says.

It *does* sound fun. But then Yvonne reminds us there's another choice.

🎵 *Turn to page 51.*

*m*y legs want to follow Dwayne right out that door. I can still feel the tingle from that jam session, and I want to know more about this Motown music.

Mrs. Porter puts her hand on her hip. "I know that look," she says, smiling. "That's a girl who's feeling like a trip to Motown."

I grin, relieved that she's not upset.

"Okay, then," says Melody. "We're coming with you, Dwayne." She seems happy about the decision, too.

"All right," says Dwayne. "Your chariot will be back to pick you up after dinner." He gives an exaggerated bow and then trots down the steps toward his car, a long brown sedan with more than a few dents and scratches on it.

The car starts up with a choke and a cough. "Some chariot!" says Melody. "Dwayne's new car is a little scary. But you're going to *love* the studio." Then she checks the clock and says, "Oh, my TV show's on!" She races across the living room.

The television is big and brown, with buttons running down one side of the screen like a microwave. It has two long metal rods coming out of the top, like the

antennae on my dad's old radio.

Melody turns a knob on the front of the TV. At first, there's nothing to see. It takes a while for the picture to appear on the screen, and when it does, it's in black and white. Melody turns another knob and flips past a few channels before she stops. "Here it is," she says, plopping down on the floor and patting the rug. "Sit by me."

A man is playing the piano and singing. The show is kind of spotty and hard to see, as if I were watching it through a snowstorm. But the music sounds really good.

The show reminds me of the ones I watch at home, where singers and musicians compete to be the next big star. Anika and I watch them and dream of the day when we'll both make it big. *She has a better chance than I do,* I think, wishing I had Anika's voice.

As three glamorous black women file onstage, Melody sits up. "The Supremes!" she says. "Oh, I hope they play my song. Please, please, please." She clasps her hands as if she's begging for a treat.

One of the women stands in front of the other two and starts to sing.

As the other women join in, Melody squeals and jumps to her feet. "Yes!" she says. "I love this song. Don't you?"

The song sounds familiar, but I don't know what it is. Melody sure does. She sings with her hand by her chin, as if she were holding a microphone. "C'mon, sing with me," she says, waving me to my feet.

"But I don't know the words," I say, panicking.

"That's okay," Melody says. "Just *ooh* and dance." She points to the TV. Two of the singers are swaying from side to side as they sing. Then they circle their arms overhead.

Even if I just *ooh*, I don't want Melody to hear my voice. What if she thinks it's terrible?

🎵 *Turn to page 52.*

he sun hangs low in the sky as we step into Big Momma's backyard after dinner.

"Taste this," says Melody's grandpa, whom she calls "Poppa." He plucks a cherry tomato off the vine for me.

I'm so full from Big Momma's chicken dinner that I can barely eat another bite. When the tomato bursts in my mouth, though, its juice tastes so sweet! "Yum," I say, forgetting not to talk with my mouth full.

"You should taste the ones Melody grows at her house," says Poppa, stroking his silver beard. "She's got dirt under her fingernails, just like I do."

I glance at Melody's fingernails, but they're clean.

She laughs. "He just means I love to garden," she says. "Poppa owns a flower shop, and he helped me and my Junior Block Club plant flowers and a vegetable garden at a park in our neighborhood. It's been a lot of work, but it sure looks great."

"I'd like to see it," I say. I can tell that gardening is one of Melody's "passions," as my dad would say. And I wonder again, *What's mine?*

As Melody bites down on a tomato, juice squirts out. "Oops!" She clamps a hand over her mouth.

"You girls better not mess up your clothes out

there," calls Big Momma from the back door. "Miss Dorothy will be here any minute to pick us up."

Melody and I smother giggles as she wipes the juice off her chin. Then we hear the doorbell ring.

"She's here," says Melody, running up the steps.

"No good-bye hug, Little One?" calls Poppa in his booming voice.

Melody stops mid-step and turns around. "Oh, sorry, Poppa," she says, racing back and wrapping her arms around his middle. "I wish you were coming with us."

"Oh, I'm much too tired," he says. "I'll just sing to myself out here in the garden." He winks at me as I wave good-bye.

🎵 *Turn to page 54.*

*w*e also need volunteers to stuff envelopes," Yvonne says. "We'll join some other youth groups at a meeting hall downtown. We want to get the word out to vote for Conyers."

Conyers? I don't know who that is. But I've stuffed plenty of envelopes for my dad's campaign. It's easy, and it would leave Melody and me time to talk. *But so would making posters,* I remind myself.

"Either one sounds like fun," Melody says. "You choose."

🎵 *To make posters,*
turn to page 66.

🎵 *To stuff envelopes,*
turn to page 56.

ooh quietly and sway along to the music.

Luckily, the TV is loud. And Melody's beautiful voice drowns mine out. Suddenly, she darts toward the dining room. When she comes back, she's holding two bananas from the fruit bowl—one like a microphone in her hand, and another one for me.

Every time I sing into that banana, it cracks me up. By the time the song ends, we're both out of breath and laughing.

"That was really fun," Melody says. "I love The Supremes. Did you know that Dwayne actually *knows* Diana Ross, the lead singer?"

"No way!" I say. I've heard that name before, which means Diana Ross must be a big star. She does seem really elegant and has an amazing voice.

"Well," says Melody, "they're not like best friends or anything. But we saw Miss Ross at Hudson's department store in February, and she waved at Dwayne!"

"Gosh," I say, "I've imagined meeting Zoey Gatz lots of times. But I don't think it'll ever happen."

"Zoey Gatz?" asks Melody, her forehead creasing.

Oops! Of course Melody doesn't know Zoey Gatz. But if she lived in my time, she would. Zoey is *always*

on the cover of magazines. "She's . . . pretty new," I say. "My mom doesn't think she's all that great, but I like her."

"Why doesn't your mom like her?" asks Melody, cocking her head.

"She's kind of rude to reporters," I say. "She sometimes gets into trouble. Mom says she 'makes bad choices.'" I do my best impersonation of Mom when I say those words.

As Melody laughs, I wonder, *Will Zoey Gatz be famous for a long time, just like Diana Ross?* I'm not so sure.

When Mrs. Porter pushes through the kitchen door carrying a stack of plates, she says, "Speaking of choices, are you girls going to eat those bananas, or just sing the life out of 'em?"

I whirl around to face Melody. *Did Mrs. Porter see us dancing and singing like that? How embarrassing!*

Melody and I start laughing again. Then she shrugs and delivers our bananas back to the fruit bowl.

🎵 *Turn to page 59.*

*m*iss Dorothy's car doesn't have seat belts either.

I try not to think about that as we cruise down 12th Street toward the performance hall.

"There's Poppa's flower shop," Melody says, pointing. The words "Frank's Flowers" stand out against the darkened windows of the shop.

A few minutes later, we slow down in front of an old brick building. The hall doesn't look fancy from the outside, but as soon as we step inside, I feel a shiver of excitement. The walls of the entryway are lined with photographs of performers, and some of them look really glamorous and professional. Other photos show groups of kids onstage.

"Are you in one of these pictures?" I ask Melody, remembering that her choir sang here once.

"Maybe!" she says, her eyes scanning the wall. But as musicians begin tuning their instruments from the stage at the back of the room, Miss Dorothy and Big Momma wave us on to find a seat.

When we're about halfway down the row of chairs, a woman calls out, "Dorothy! Geneva!" The woman steps off the stage and hurries over. She's tall and slender, with black hair piled high atop her head. "I'm so

glad you're here," she says, wrapping them in a hug.

"Ah, Josephine," says Miss Dorothy. "It's been too long."

Then Josephine smiles warmly at Melody and me. "I'm so glad you brought a friend," she says to Melody.

"Me, too," Melody says, squeezing my hand before introducing me to Josephine.

"Where's that husband of yours?" Big Momma asks Josephine.

"He's around here somewhere," says Josephine. "And he's *thrilled* that you could make it tonight." She gestures toward the stage. "Come with me. We have front-row seats for you."

I follow Melody. The stage is so close! If I reached out my hand, I could almost touch it. There's a saxophone player warming up onstage, plus a guitar player, a drummer, and a man seated at a huge piano.

By the time the lights dim even more, the tables around us have filled with people. Big Momma raises a finger to her lips. The show's about to start!

♪ *Turn to page 62.*

*Y*vonne drives Melody and me to a meeting hall downtown. When we get there, I'm surprised by how many volunteers—young and old—are already in the room. Signs on the walls read "Elect John Conyers Jr. for Congress."

"Congress? My dad was elected to Congress!" I say under my breath.

But Melody hears me. "That's really cool!" she says. "What does your dad do?"

Oh, man, I think, because I don't really know what to say. I mumble something about him trying to create more jobs and "make sure people get paid enough."

Melody nods. "That's important," she says. "If people don't earn enough money, they have to work twice as hard—double shifts sometimes. Daddy has to work those at the auto factory, so he's gone a lot."

Her words linger in my head as we take seats at a long table. I never thought about it that way—that what my dad does matters for families like Melody's.

We tag-team to stuff the envelopes. I fold the fly-ers, and Melody slides them into envelopes. The work is kind of boring, until Yvonne whispers, "Don't look now. You'll never believe who's here!"

"Ouch!" Yvonne's announcement surprises me right into a paper cut. As I suck my finger, I do exactly what Yvonne told me not to do. I turn around and look. There's an older woman with glasses sitting nearby, a polka-dot umbrella hanging from the back of her chair.

"It's Mrs. Rosa Parks," Yvonne whispers.

Rosa Parks! Anika wrote a report about her for history class last year. Rosa Parks is the black woman who refused to give up her seat on a bus to a white person. Anika said people call her "the mother of the civil rights movement."

"Is she really stuffing envelopes, just like us?" asks Melody.

"Sure she is," says Yvonne. "She lives here in Detroit now. Did you think she was still sitting on a bus somewhere? She's out here all the time, working with young people and for politicians, getting things done behind the scenes."

I can't believe Rosa Parks is here. Our work just got a whole lot more interesting—and feels more important, too.

"Should we talk to her?" asks Melody after a few minutes of watching.

Should we? I wonder. The thought of talking to Rosa Parks makes my heart race. But I wait too long to decide. Suddenly, Mrs. Parks pushes away from the table and stands up. Is she leaving?

Sure enough, Mrs. Parks says a few good-byes and heads for the door.

As soon as she's gone, Melody slumps down in her chair. "I can't believe we didn't say a single word to her," she says.

"I know, but what would we have said? My tongue would have been tied in knots," I admit.

Melody sighs. "Mine, too."

That's when I see the umbrella still hanging from Mrs. Parks's chair. "Melody, look," I say, pointing.

"Her umbrella!" she says. "Should we go after her?"

"Go after who?" asks Yvonne, sliding into the empty seat next to me.

To run after Mrs. Parks, turn to page 65.

To tell Yvonne about the umbrella, turn to page 61.

*A*fter dinner, we hear Dwayne's car chug to a stop out front. Before he can even ring the doorbell, Melody and I are halfway out the door.

As we slide into the backseat, Melody says, "I wonder if we'll see anybody famous at the studio. Maybe The Temptations . . ." she says, her eyes hopeful.

"Or The Supremes?" I add, happy that I finally know some of the Motown stars.

"Or The Three Ravens?" asks Dwayne, winking at us in his rearview mirror.

Melody giggles. At first, I don't get the joke. Then I remember that Dwayne's band is called The Three Ravens.

When the car backfires, Melody says, "What I *really* wonder is whether we're even going to make it to the studio in this car. Are we leaving a trail of smoke?" As she turns to look out the back window, Melody catches my eye and grins.

Dwayne chuckles. "She's old, all right," he says. "But as soon as my album starts selling, I'll buy something newer. Maybe a Ford Mustang like those rich producers down at the studio drive."

"Ooh," says Melody. "A Mustang!" She must know

her cars, because her eyes light up.

"That's right," says Dwayne, puffing out his chest proudly. Then the car backfires again, and he smacks the steering wheel and sinks back down in his seat, laughing with us.

Turn to page 68.

*m*elody isn't exactly leaping out of her chair to get the umbrella, and I hang back, too. What would we say to Rosa Parks even if we caught up with her? Instead, we tell Yvonne about the umbrella.

"Ah," she says. "I'll make sure it finds its way back to her."

But as Melody and I go back to stuffing envelopes, I keep thinking: *Did we just miss out on something big?* Our work isn't nearly as exciting anymore. So when Yvonne tells us it's time to do something else, we're ready.

"You two can help me with voter registration," she says as we get into the car. "We'll go door to door, making sure people know how to sign up to vote."

Door to door? Like we're selling cookies or magazines? I was never very good at that.

"Like you did in Mississippi?" Melody asks. She looks nervous. Is she afraid we'll get arrested the way Yvonne did? My stomach lurches at the thought.

♫ *Turn to page 71.*

Four women come out onto the stage. As one of them steps to the microphone, silence falls over the audience. Then the piano player begins.

"Why should I feel discouraged?" the woman sings in a deep, soulful voice. *"No, no, no . . ."* She shakes her finger at us. *"Why should the shadows come?"*

A couple of people in the audience start to clap. Melody and I turn to face each other. We know the song, too! My grandma taught it to me. My fingers tap out the notes on my lap as the refrain begins.

> *I sing because I'm happy,*
> *I sing because I'm free,*
> *For His eye is on the sparrow,*
> *And I know He watches me.*

The other women onstage are singing now, too, standing behind the lead singer.

> *Watches over me,*
> *I'm so glad that He,*
> *Watches over me,*
> *I'm so glad that He . . .*

All around the room, the crowd sways in time to the music, like one great congregation. When we first got here, I was afraid that listening to this kind of music without Grammy would make me feel sad. But it actually makes me feel like she's right here beside me.

When the song ends, Big Momma and Miss Dorothy stand up and applaud, so Melody and I jump up, too. I lean close to Melody. "That was beautiful," I whisper. She smiles at me and claps louder.

The lead singer laughs and bows her head, sweat glistening on her forehead. Then she nods to the guitar player, and they begin again.

Every song is just as incredible as the last. I don't know them all, but I sure want to. After about five or six songs, a man steps onstage, and the crowd cheers. Is he another musician?

"There's Al," whispers Miss Dorothy, nudging Big Momma.

Al must be Josephine's husband, the owner of the performance hall. He raises his hands to quiet the crowd. "Thank you for coming out for this very special performance," he says in a deep, friendly voice.

He clears his throat and then continues. "As most

of you know, this will be our last performance here. On Monday, the city will start turning this old building into your newest paved parking lot."

What? Melody whirls around to face me.

🎵 *Turn to page 76.*

*w*e'll be right back!" I say, jumping up. I grab the umbrella, and Melody races after me out the front door.

At the base of the steps, we look both ways. The sidewalk is empty. "She's gone," I say, my stomach sinking. Then I see her—about to turn the corner. "This way!" I cry.

We sprint down the sidewalk. But as we get closer to Mrs. Parks, I wonder again: *What will we say to her? How do you talk to your hero?*

At the sound of our footsteps, Mrs. Parks turns around. "Oh, my umbrella! Thank you, girls. You're so kind."

She's not much taller than we are, but I feel like I'm looking up to her. The sun over her shoulders is blinding.

Say something! says the voice in my head. My palms are sweating, but my mouth is bone dry.

🎵 *Turn to page 74.*

*m*elody and I decide to stay at the church and make posters. We sit at a card table, stenciling big letters onto poster board.

"How's this?" asks Melody, holding up her sign. It reads "DOWN WITH DISCRIMINATION."

"That's really good!" I say, noticing how evenly spaced her letters are. "Have you done this before?"

Melody reaches for a pot of paint. "I made signs for the Walk to Freedom last year," she says. "And I made signs when we picketed at Fieldston's Clothing Store this year. The people who work there weren't very nice to black people." Her face hardens. "The manager accused my brother and me of shoplifting and told us to leave."

For a moment, I'm speechless. "They kicked you out?" I finally say. "That's so unfair. Did the picketing do any good?"

Melody nods and begins to paint in the letters on her poster. "It took a while. We started in February. We handed out leaflets explaining how Fieldston's treated black customers. People stopped shopping there, and Fieldston's lost money." Melody smiles. "The store's manager has finally agreed to change things."

"Wow," I say, amazed. "So picketing the store made things better?"

"It didn't happen right away," says Melody, "but what we did made things better." Then she looks at my poster board and says, "Your sign is really good, too."

I stenciled "JUSTICE NOW" on my sign, because I saw another girl do that. My letters aren't as perfect as Melody's, but after I fill them in with paint, they look a lot nicer.

Then Melody and I add our own touches to the signs. She adds arrows pointing downward to go with the slogan "DOWN WITH DISCRIMINATION." I underline the "NOW!" on my sign with a rainbow of stripes.

We make more signs, too. By the time we're done, my hands are smudged with paint.

"Nice work, you two," says Yvonne. "Now can I ask a favor? I've got to get these signs to a friend's shop a few blocks away. Can you help me carry them?"

Melody and I agree to help. That's before we find out how heavy the signs are—and how *hot* it is outside. We can hardly wait to get to the shop!

🎵 *Turn to page 79.*

I expected the record studio to be in a big office building. Instead, the Motown studio looks like a small house with two front doors and a big picture window between them. A sign over the window reads "Hitsville U.S.A." Excitement ripples through my body. *Will we hear some hits tonight?* I wonder.

As Melody and I follow Dwayne through one of the doors, a teenage guy greets us. "Well, well," he says, "if it isn't Miss Melody Ellison herself. Long time no see, lil sis."

Melody grins. "Hey, Artie," she says. "Artie's one of The Three Ravens," she tells me. "And Phil is the other one."

I meet Phil, too, after Artie leads us through a maze of rooms and hallways into the rehearsal room. I'm surprised to see a drummer and a piano player warming up beside Phil. "Wait, I thought there were only three Ravens," I whisper to Melody.

"Those two musicians are part of Motown's house band, the Funk Brothers," she explains. "They play during recordings and rehearsals. They're really good—those guys can play *anything*."

I watch the man at the piano. He does seem super

talented. I try to imagine recording a song with the musicians here at Hitsville. My stomach flip-flops at the thought, knowing that the recorded song would be heard by millions of people . . .

Dwayne snaps his fingers, breaking my daydream. "Okay, let's do it," he says to his bandmates. "Show's in three days."

The Three Ravens line up in a row. As the drummer finds a beat, Dwayne steps forward and begins to croon in his high voice. Behind him, Artie and Phil dance, moving like mirror images of each other.

"Give it a chance, girl," sings Dwayne. *"Just one chance."*

Artie and Phil each lift their pointer fingers like the number one. Then they spin in a circle and sing, *"Just one . . . just one . . ."*

Melody sings and sways along from her chair beside me. I'm not the only one who notices, because after The Three Ravens finish, Artie says, "I think we could use a couple more backup singers." He strokes his chin.

"That's right," says Dwayne, catching on. "The Temptations usually have five singers. How come we

only have three? What do you say, Melody?"

She's instantly up and standing beside Artie and Phil, but my bottom is glued to the chair. As they all stare at me, my face starts to burn.

"C'mon," says Melody. "It'll be fun. It's your chance to sing at an actual recording studio!"

Dwayne starts singing to me, *"Give it a chance, girl. Just one chance."*

My cheek twitches, and I smile nervously. It would be pretty cool, but I'm not a very good singer.

Then Artie, Phil, and Melody add, *"Just one."*

I laugh, but my stomach is still flip-flopping like a fish. I finally stand up, mostly so that they'll all stop singing to me! *Just sing softly,* I think as I take my place in line. *Like you did at Mrs. Porter's when The Supremes were on TV.*

So I do, whispering the words. And soon I get lost in the swirl of voices around me. But as the song comes to an end, I realize what I'm actually doing. *I'm singing with Motown stars at Hitsville U.S.A.—a real recording studio!* And now I'm grinning like crazy.

🎵 **Turn to page 83.**

"I'm not sure about this voter-registration thing," Melody whispers. "I wish Yvonne had given us a choice to do something else."

Yvonne overhears from the driver's seat. She purses her lips and then says, "You mean, you didn't get to vote on something that mattered to you, Melody? How'd that feel?"

Melody hangs her head, as if she just got caught talking in class. "Not good."

"Right. So you see what I'm saying?" says Yvonne. "We have to make sure people can vote. Remember, Daddy always says that voting is like having a voice. Everyone should have a voice about things that matter to them."

"But, Yvonne," Melody says softly. "Your wrist . . ."

Understanding spreads across Yvonne's face. "Oh, I see," she says. "Are you girls scared?"

Melody nods. "Why aren't you?" she asks.

Yvonne straightens up in her seat. "Because when I was sitting in that jail, I told myself that I wasn't going to let fear hold me back. I don't want you to either, Dee-Dee. No matter where we are, we can't let fear keep us from doing what's right. Do you understand?"

Melody nods and sits a little taller.

Through the window beside her, I see a tall concrete wall built along the road. It seems to stretch on for miles. "What's that?" I ask Yvonne.

She glances out the window. "That was built by developers who wanted to keep white neighborhoods separate from black neighborhoods. It's six feet high and about a foot thick."

"They built an actual *wall*?" I say.

"A big, ugly concrete wall," Melody says. "It looks like it's crumbling in parts, though."

Yvonne shakes her head. "It's still much too strong. There are still lines drawn between white neighborhoods and black neighborhoods, even if there aren't actual walls built between all of them."

"Like my cousin Val's neighborhood," Melody tells me. "It's mostly white, and it was hard for her family to buy their house. Some of the neighbors didn't want them there. But they finally found someone to sell to them."

Yvonne glances in the rearview mirror. "Did you help Val plant flowers at her new place yet, Dee-Dee?"

"Yes!" she says. Then she turns to me. "You should

see them. Wait, maybe you can. Maybe Mommy will let us go to Val's tomorrow."

"That sounds fun," I say. And we could use some fun right now, after hearing about how badly Melody's cousin and other black families are being treated.

🎵 *Turn to page 86.*

efore I lose my nerve, I say, "Mrs. Parks, you're my role model."

She smiles warmly. "Thank you. I hope you have *many* role models, as I do," she says. "Even people who are much younger than I am. You know, I'm learning all the time from the young people in my neighborhood block club."

"I started a block club, too!" Melody says excitedly. "Well, a Junior Block Club. We fixed up a playground and planted a vegetable garden. I really like to garden."

"Is that right?" says Mrs. Parks. "Starting a block club is a lot like gardening: planting a seed and watching it grow. My brother is a gardener, too, and I enjoy helping him harvest and can those fresh vegetables."

Beside me, Melody is about bursting with pride now.

"Thank you for this," says Mrs. Parks again, raising her umbrella. "Not that I'll be needing it on what turned into such a beautiful day." Before she walks away, she says, "You're never too young to be a role model—remember that, girls. Anyone can be a leader. We're all leaders of *something*. Start leading, and others will follow." Then she turns the corner . . . and is gone.

We're all leaders of something. Mrs. Parks's words bounce around in my head as Melody and I walk back to the meeting hall.

"You should be proud," I say to Melody. "You're already a leader, with your Junior Block Club and your gardening." But then I think, *What am I a leader of? Can I be a role model, too?*

🎵 **Turn to page 81.**

ℬ ig Momma and Miss Dorothy don't seem surprised by Al's news—they must have known
already.

"It's part of Detroit's 'urban renewal' project,"
Big Momma explains while the band takes a break.
"Sometimes when the city's leaders decide to build new
freeways or parking lots, they tear down the old businesses that we love. And homes, too. Al and Josephine
live in the apartment upstairs," she says, pointing
upward. "Urban renewal seems to hit colored folks'
homes and businesses the hardest."

Melody sighs. "We talked about urban renewal at
our last Junior Block Club meeting. When homes are
torn down, sometimes beautiful gardens are ruined,
too." She slumps in her seat.

Big Momma pats Melody's hand. "What's important
to you and me isn't always what's important to others,
baby," she says. "Like music. Remember what I told you
about the part of Detroit called Paradise Valley? Some
of the finest musicians performed there. But the city
built a freeway, and they bulldozed Paradise Valley to
make room for it."

Miss Dorothy shakes her head sadly. "I remember

seeing Ella Fitzgerald perform at the Forest Club. Or was it the Horseshoe Lounge? There were so many clubs, and restaurants and hotels, too—almost all owned by colored people. It was like we had our own city within a city. Oh, there was such energy there!" She shivers, as if she can still feel it.

"I saw Billie Holiday in Paradise Valley. That woman could *sing*," says Big Momma. "But after the I-75 freeway came on through, it was all gone. The businesses. The music. The magic. All of it."

A knot forms in my stomach. The last time I felt this way was when Mom said we wouldn't have guitars for music class. *Why don't people care about music?* I want to holler. *Or gardens? Or people's businesses?* I wish I could *do* something.

"Why the long faces?" asks Josephine, pulling up a chair. "Are you all worrying about Al and me? Don't you be doing that, now."

Big Momma forces a smile. "You two are going to land on your feet," she says encouragingly. "But you're losing your home, aren't you, Jo? Where will you go?"

"We're moving in with our daughter, at least for a while," says Josephine. "We'll spend some time with

our grandbabies." Then a shadow passes over her face, and she says, "You know, I think it's our old piano that Al is going to miss the most."

"Aren't you taking it with you?" I ask shyly. It's hard to imagine leaving a piano behind.

"It's not worth the money to move it," Josephine explains. "Those old keys are as sticky as molasses. But it's the first time we'll be without a piano—at least until we can afford a new one." She shakes her head, as if shaking off the bad feeling. "We'll start over," she says. "We always do."

I can tell that her heart hurts. Suddenly, I wish I could talk to Dad. As a politician, he makes decisions about things that affect my hometown, and people listen to him. He'd be able to help Al and Josephine save the performance hall, wouldn't he?

Then I remind myself where I am: Detroit. 1964. *Dad isn't here,* I realize sadly. But is there something that *I* can do?

Turn to page 90.

*A*s soon as we drop off the signs, Melody says, "I'm hot, Vonnie. And *really* thirsty."

Yvonne glances down the street. There's a sign for Sam's Soda Shop on the corner. "How about there?" she asks. "I'll buy you girls a soda for your help today."

Melody looks tempted but then shakes her head. "Not there," she says.

Why not? I want to ask. I can taste the ice-cold soda already.

"Mommy won't go there," Melody explains. "She was treated badly by a white waitress once."

Yvonne stops walking. "Is that so?" she says, arching an eyebrow. "Mom never mentioned that to me."

Melody's mouth clamps shut. "Well . . ." she begins, "that's probably because she knew you'd go in there and make a scene. You're not going to, are you, Vonnie?"

Yvonne stares at Melody, as if trying to figure out what to do. "Do you want a soda or not?" she finally asks. "Because if you do, Dee-Dee, we should go in. It's important to take a stand on things like this. Someone has to fight for what's right."

Then Yvonne turns to me and asks, "What do you

think? Should we try to make a difference here? Or would you rather keep walking?"

Help! I catch Melody's eye, but she looks just as unsure as I feel.

♪ *To keep walking,*
   turn to page 104.

♪ *To go into the shop,*
   turn to page 93.

T hat night, Melody and I stay up way too late talking about Rosa Parks. I can't stop thinking about what Mrs. Parks said about role models and leaders, and about how my dad's always encouraging me to get involved in the things I care about. I don't think I'll ever fall asleep, but suddenly, it's Monday morning.

"Wake up," says Melody, nudging me. "It's time to go meet the bookmobile."

"The what?" I ask, yawning.

"It's like a library on wheels," says Melody. "Lila and I just found out about it this summer. We go meet it every Monday morning." She grabs a book bag out of her closet.

After I'm dressed, we hurry downstairs, where Lila is just finishing her cereal.

"Bookmobile time?" asks Melody's mom, sipping her coffee. "Take the dog, too, please. He could use some fresh air."

When we get outside, Bo takes the lead, sniffing every bush along the sidewalk.

Lila's behind us with an open book. "Slow down, Melody," she scolds.

"Stop reading," Melody retorts. "Then you'll be able to keep up. And anyway, haven't you read that book a thousand times already?"

Lila shrugs. "Yvonne says we should read more books by black authors," she says. "And this is the only one that the bookmobile has."

I see the author's name on the cover: Langston Hughes. "Hey, I know about him," I say. "My mom gave me a book of his poems."

"I have one of his books, too," says Melody. "He signed it at Hudson's downtown."

"No way!" I would *love* to meet a real author. Then I realize what Lila said a minute ago. "Wait . . . the bookmobile has only one book by a black author?"

Lila nods, and Melody doesn't look at all surprised.

I own lots of books written by black authors—Mom even helped me write a letter to one of them once. But would Lila recognize any of those authors' names? Were their books even around in 1964?

I don't know, so I keep my mouth shut.

♫ *Turn to page 88.*

(T) he Three Ravens are halfway through their
third song when a woman pokes her head into
the room. "Are you ready to head across the street?"
she asks.

Dwayne checks the clock and says, "Yeah, we'd
better wrap it up here."

"What's across the street?" I ask Melody.

"Artist Development," she says. "It's like a school
where musicians learn about everything *besides*
music—like how to dress, how to dance, how to act,
how to talk to reporters . . ."

"Really?" I say. "They learn all that?"

Melody nods. "Motown stars do. That's why they
look so polished. Remember The Supremes on TV?"

I do. Maybe that's why Diana Ross looked so
elegant and graceful. She'd taken lessons!

My mind flashes to a poster of Zoey Gatz on my
bedroom wall. She's sticking out her tongue, which
I always thought was kind of funny. But she sure
doesn't look very "polished."

A few minutes later, Melody and I are watching a
man with a gray beard teach The Three Ravens *chor-
eography,* a fancy word for "dancing." Artie and Phil

are practicing their footwork, crossing one foot over the other and spinning in a low circle. When Artie wobbles, I expect him to laugh at himself. But he doesn't. He's working really hard.

I turn to say so to Melody, but she's gone. She's standing in the doorway, watching something across the hall. When I join her, I can see into the other room, too. A woman with a friendly face is coaching a teen-age girl on how to walk gracefully.

"Do you know that girl?" I ask, wondering if she's famous.

"Not yet," says Melody. "But maybe we will *someday.*"

I try to memorize the girl's face. When I get home, I'll look up Motown stars online. Will I find her there?

"Stand taller," the woman says. "Show that you respect yourself. Then other people will respect you, too."

"Wow," I whisper. "That's what my grammy used to say."

Just then, Dwayne steps into the hall and says, "I've got to run an errand for one of the producers. Wanna join me? We'll be cruisin' in a brand-new Mustang."

He holds up a set of shiny keys.

Melody's eyes light up. "I've never ridden in a Mustang before," she says. Then she glances back at the girl taking lessons on how to be a superstar. "But we're having fun here, too."

She turns to me. "What should we do?"

🎵 To stay at the studio,
turn to page 101.

🎵 To go with Dwayne,
turn to page 95.

On Monday morning, as Melody's mother turns the car into Val's neighborhood, I press my face up against the window. Tall trees shade the street, and lawns stretch out long and green in front of the houses. "It looks so different from the neighborhood we visited yesterday with Yvonne," I say.

Registering voters took us through a black neighborhood where kids played outside on the steps and sidewalks. There's much more space to play here, in Val's new neighborhood, but I don't see as many kids.

"Has Val made any friends yet?" I ask, craning my neck to watch a boy coast down his driveway on a blue bike.

Melody shakes her head. "I don't think so, and she and her parents moved in a few months ago."

As we turn into Val's driveway, the front door of the house bursts open. A tall girl a little older than me hurries down the steps. "You're here!" she says, hugging Melody.

She introduces herself to me and then gestures toward the backyard. "Daddy just put up a swing set," she says. "Want to come see?"

"Go ahead, girls," says Melody's mom. "I'm going

to go inside and visit with Cousin Tish."

We follow Val along the fenceline toward the back-yard. When a blonde woman with a sun hat pops up on the other side of the fence, Melody takes a quick step backward in surprise.

"Oh, hello!" she says to the woman, who is wearing gardening gloves. But the woman must not have heard her because she bends back down without saying anything.

There's a girl sitting on the porch behind the woman. She's blonde, too, with a high ponytail. I wave at the girl, but she immediately looks away.

"My mom says our neighbors aren't used to having black families on their block," Val says quietly.

Val's neighbors won't even talk to her? I wonder. *That's so wrong!*

When I glance back at the blonde girl, she's looking at me again, too. She may not be talking to us, but she sure seems curious.

 *Turn to page 99.*

(T)he bookmobile looks like a long white ice cream truck, with a short line of kids waiting to get in. When we reach the entrance, Melody and I stay outside with Bo while Lila steps inside.

When it's our turn to board the bookmobile, I'm amazed: I feel like I'm in a real library, standing between two shelves of books! While Melody searches one shelf, I step toward the other one.

"Can I help you find something?" asks the librarian, who is white.

I'm about to say "No, thanks." But then I decide to speak up. "Do you have any books by black authors?" I ask.

"We do have one that was just returned," she says. "Poetry by Mr. Langston Hughes. Have you heard of him?"

My hopes sink. I've heard of him, all right. But that book can't be the *only* one. "Do you have any others?" I ask.

The librarian shakes her head sadly. "Publishers don't put out enough books by Negro authors." She smiles and adds, "It does my heart good to see you asking for them, though. If enough people asked,

(w)hen we get back to her house, Big Momma makes a bed for me on her couch and another one on the rug for Melody. My new friend and I are having a Saturday night sleepover. But as Big Momma turns out the lights, Melody seems sad and far away.

"I wish we could help Auntie Josephine and Uncle Al save the performance hall," she whispers into the darkness. She loves music as much as I do.

I have weird dreams all night. I dream that I'm performing onstage at the hall with my brand-new guitar, and I don't feel the slightest bit nervous! But then the front door opens and cars start zooming into the room—as if a freeway were running right through it. And after the last car passes by, I glance down and realize that my guitar is gone.

When I finally open my eyes to the morning light, Melody is awake, too.

"I didn't get much sleep last night," she says, fighting a huge yawn.

"Me, neither," I confess. "I'm so worried about the performance hall."

Melody nods sadly. "I think we should talk to my sister Yvonne. She'll know what to do."

Just then, Big Momma bursts through the kitchen door with a towel draped over her shoulder. "Good morning, my chicks," she sings. "Come and have some breakfast before church."

Melody nods as another yawn sneaks up on her.

"Are you feeling okay, baby?" asks Big Momma. She leans over to put a hand against Melody's forehead.

"We just didn't sleep well," says Melody. "We were worrying about Uncle Al and Auntie Josephine."

Big Momma straightens back up. "I'm worrying about them, too. But I have an idea that might make you feel better. After church, your cousin Val and her parents are driving to Windsor for the Emancipation Celebration. How would you girls like to go, too?"

"Mancipation?" I ask.

"*E*-mancipation," Big Momma corrects me. "It means 'freedom'—of the slaves in our country and in other parts of the world. The Emancipation Celebration is a celebration of our freedom."

"It's in Canada, just across the Detroit River," says Melody. "Because that's where the Underground Railroad ended and slaves from the South found freedom, right, Big Momma?"

"That's right," says Big Momma.

"There's this giant parade," says Melody, spreading her hands. "Plus a pet show, a beauty contest, and lots of music."

"Four choirs performing, in fact," Big Momma adds.

"And don't forget the barbecued spareribs!" says Poppa, coming down the stairs.

Melody laughs. "You like barbecue as much as Daddy does—and that's a *lot*."

Poppa holds his palms up. "Guilty as charged," he booms good-naturedly.

"So is that a yes?" asks Big Momma.

Melody turns to me and says, "It'd be great if you could meet my cousin, Val." Then the spark fades from her eyes. "But if we go, we won't have time to figure out how to help Uncle Al and Auntie Josephine."

"I know," I whisper sadly.

🎵 **To try to help Al and Josephine,
turn to page 98.**

🎵 **To go to the celebration,
go online to beforever.com/endings**

I think about Dad's campaign manager, Mr. Chapman, who was mistaken for a valet just because of the color of his skin. I think of Melody and her brother, who were asked to leave Fieldston's because they were black. Then I think about how hurt Melody looked when she talked about that.

I know in my head—and heart—what to do. I take a deep breath. "I think we should go in," I say, hoping Melody isn't mad at me.

She doesn't look mad—only a little scared, maybe. But she nods and says, "I think we should, too."

Yvonne puts a hand on my shoulder. "Good for you, girls," she tells us. "That's a brave decision."

I don't feel brave, though, as I follow her into the shop. The bell above the door jingles, and my mind starts racing. *Will the waitresses be mean to us? Will they make us leave?*

Melody stands close to me just inside the door. The waitress at the cash register glances up but then quickly looks away. The letters on her name tag read "SUE."

Yvonne clears her throat, but Sue turns her back on us. Without a word, the waitress grabs a pitcher of

water and starts working her way down a row of tables.

"What do we do now?" whispers Melody. "I don't think she's coming back!"

Yvonne's mouth is set in a determined line. "We wait," she says.

Turn to page 108.

It smells so *new*," I say, climbing into the back of the Mustang. Everything in the car is red, from the leather seats to the steering wheel.

"That's because it *is* new," says Melody. "A 1964 Ford Mustang! Daddy says it's the most popular car of the year. Dwayne, turn on the radio."

"You got it," he says. He starts the engine and reaches for the radio.

As soon as the music flows through the speakers, Melody recognizes the song. "The Temptations!" she says. "Turn it up louder."

Dwayne does. Then he adjusts his mirrors and rolls down his window halfway. "Pretty soon, Dee-Dee," he says as he eases away from the curb, "you're going to be hearing a lot more of me when you turn on the radio." He looks proud as a peacock sitting up there.

"I know," says Melody. "And then people will be running errands for *you*."

"They'll treat you like a king," I add. The pop stars I know are even more famous than kings and queens. The last time I saw Zoey Gatz on TV, she was walking down a royal red carpet at an awards show.

Dwayne chuckles. "Right," he says. "All except for

that 'king' part. I don't care if you're The Temptations or Smokey Robinson himself. No black musician is treated like a king on the road, especially in the South."

Melody nods solemnly. Then she tells me, "Dwayne went on tour down South, and he said the black musicians couldn't stay in the same hotels as white people. They couldn't use the front doors of clubs, either, because those were for white people. They had to go in the back."

"Really?" I say, trying to understand. Zoey Gatz is black, but I can't imagine a hotel ever turning her away.

Suddenly, a siren swells behind us, and red and blue flashing lights pour through the back window.

🎶 *Turn to page 113.*

*A*fter Melody chooses her books, we step back outside. The line of kids has grown now, snaking around the corner.

"Ready to go?" asks Lila.

Melody nods, but my feet are frozen to the sidewalk. Most of the kids waiting in this line are black. *Don't they want to read books by black authors?* I wonder.

"We have to do something," I say.

"What do you mean?" asks Melody, confused.

"The librarian said that more kids have to ask for books by black authors," I explain. "Then she'll start a petition to send to the publishers. We have to get kids to ask for those books." *But how?* I think about the ways my dad spreads the word when he's campaigning. He uses the Internet: making videos, posting on blogs, and e-mailing people. But I can't do any of that in Melody's time. There's no Internet. There aren't even any computers.

Suddenly, Bo barks, as if to say, "Speak!"

"That's it!" I say. I don't need the Internet. I can spread the word using my own voice.

♫ *Turn to page 103.*

*w*hen Melody and I decide to stay home, Big
Momma pulls us both into a hug. "It's hard to
celebrate when people we care about are hurting," she
says. "But going to church will help our hearts, and so
will having family over for Sunday dinner. Doesn't that
sound good?"

Melody nods. "Yvonne will come to dinner, too,
right? I want to talk to her about the performance hall."

"Both your sisters will be coming," says Big
Momma.

"Wait, *sisters*?" I say to Melody. "You have more
than one?"

She nods. "There's Lila, too. She's a little older than
me—well, she'd say she's a *lot* older. She's kind of a
know-it-all." Melody rolls her eyes. "But that's because
she reads all the time."

Big Momma clucks her tongue. "That's enough now.
The Good Book says to love thy sisters—*all* of them."

Melody laughs. "The Bible doesn't say that!"

But Big Momma is already back in the kitchen,
chuckling to herself.

Turn to page 105.

*V*al's new swing set has a couple of yellow swings and a red glider. "You two swing first," she says, climbing onto the glider. "Wait until you see how high they go!"

Melody settles into the swing next to me and starts pumping her legs. "I can see the flowers we planted from up here," she says, her feet flying high overhead.

The only thing I can see from my swing is the girl next door. When her mom gathers her gardening tools and goes inside, the girl takes a step toward the fence.

"Do you want a turn?" I call to her.

She slowly nods. Then she walks toward the gate connecting the two lawns to each other. I wonder if it's ever been used.

I drag my feet on the grass to stop the swing, and then I hop off and hand it to the girl. "Thanks," she says shyly.

Val quickly introduces herself to the girl, who says her name is Cindy. "You can come swing anytime you want," Val says, grinning.

Cindy's face lights up. "I'd like that," she says. "Mom won't let me get a swing set of my own. She'd have to tear out some of her flowers to make room!"

Melody laughs and then challenges Cindy to a who-can-swing-higher contest. So I climb on the other side of Val's glider, and pretty soon we're seesawing back and forth, too.

"Girls!" calls a woman from the back of Val's house. It must be Cousin Tish. "Do you want some lemonade and—"

She stops talking when she catches sight of Cindy on the swing. Then Cousin Tish smiles thoughtfully and adds, "Lemonade and cookies?"

"Yes, please!" shouts Val.

Before Cousin Tish can go back inside, the blonde woman comes out of the house next door. She hurries toward the fence, her mouth open as if to call Cindy back home.

Uh-oh, I think. *This means trouble . . .*

🎵 *Turn to page 109.*

Can we stay?" I ask Melody. It's my first time at a Motown studio, and I'm pretty sure it will be my last.

Melody doesn't seem disappointed. She may like cars, but I think she likes music even more—like me.

Dwayne tosses the keys in the air and catches them as he strides down the long hallway toward the front door. But a moment later, he's back.

"What happened?" asks Melody.

"The producer found another errand boy so that I could hang back and look after you two," he says, his face long. I bet he was already picturing himself behind the wheel of that fancy car.

"Oh, sorry," says Melody, biting her lip.

"Don't worry about it," says Dwayne. "I wouldn't want to miss learning how to walk now, would I?" He grins, pointing at the women in the room. "Did you know that's Mr. Gordy's sister? She works for her brother, polishing up Motown stars till they shine."

"Really?" says Melody. Then she says playfully, "If you ever want to go into business with *me*, Dwayne, I'd be happy to teach you some manners."

Dwayne jokes right back. "That wouldn't be half

bad, little sis," he says. "Then I could be the boss of you—for real." His face grows serious, though, when he says, "There *is* something I could use your help with."

"What?" Melody asks, all ears.

Dwayne glances down the hall. "Later," he says. "I'll tell you later."

As he disappears into the rehearsal room, Melody says, "I wonder what *that* was all about."

I do, too. What's Dwayne's big secret?

Turn to page 120.

I step toward the first person in line, a boy about my age. "Ask the librarians if they have any books by black authors," I tell him. "If enough kids ask, they'll petition the publishers to print more. Pass it on."

The boy raises his eyebrows in surprise, but then he cups his hand and whispers to the girl behind him.

When Melody sees what I did, she starts talking with kids in the middle of the line. "Pass it on," she says.

Then we stand back and watch the kids whispering, each one turning toward the next. I feel huge relief—we actually did something!

Anyone can lead, Rosa Parks said to me. I'm not a politician like Dad. I'm just a girl. But like Melody and her gardening, I planted a seed, and now I'm watching it grow.

ꞋꞋ♪ *The End* ꞋꞋ♪

To read this story another way and see how different choices lead to a different ending, turn back to page 58.

I've never had a waitress be mean to me before. So I tell Melody and Yvonne the truth. "I don't really want to go into Sam's Soda Shop."

"Me either," Melody adds. "Can we go to the soda fountain at Barthwell's?" she asks Yvonne. "You always say we should give our business to shops that are owned by black people."

Yvonne sighs. "Yes. We want to support them. But, Dee-Dee, think about it: If we only shopped at those places, nothing would ever change. Businesses like this one would keep treating black people poorly. That's not okay, is it?"

Melody's shoulders sag. She shakes her head.

"Let's just go home," says Yvonne. "Mom is making food for the volunteers, and we can help her."

Melody and I are quiet on the walk back to the church. Did we disappoint Yvonne by not going into the soda shop? Maybe. *At least we can make food with Melody's mom,* I remind myself. *At least we can still help.*

🎵 *Turn to page 117.*

*A*n hour later, I'm sitting beside Melody in church, but all I can think about is Al and Josephine. While Pastor Daniels talks about helping others, I wonder, *How can Melody and I save the performance hall? We're just two girls. Two girls can't go up against a whole city!*

I can't wait for Sunday dinner—mostly because I want to meet Melody's big sister, Yvonne. Melody says Yvonne will know what to do. I hope, hope, hope she's right.

I decide I like *all* of Melody's siblings when we're back at Big Momma's house a couple of hours later. Lila is quiet but nice. And Melody was right—she does read all the time. She sneaks a book to read under the table before dinner starts. I've done that before! I catch her eye and grin.

As Dwayne taps out a rhythm on the table with his spoon, he winks at me. I still feel shy around him, knowing that he's sort of famous.

And then there's Yvonne. She rushed through the front door a minute ago, wearing a colorful scarf over her Afro. I noticed a cast on her wrist, but before I could ask Melody about it, Poppa started carrying

bowls of steaming food in from the kitchen. The delicious smell brought us all to the table.

Sitting down, surrounded by Melody's family, I suddenly feel homesick. I start thinking about my mom and dad—until I hear Melody telling Yvonne about Al and Josephine's place.

"They're going to start tearing it down tomorrow!" says Melody.

Yvonne furrows her brow. "We should stage a demonstration," she says. "I'll talk to my friends in the Student Walk to Freedom Club this afternoon. If enough of us show up and surround the building, they *can't* tear it down."

"Whoa, let's slow down," says Melody's dad from the other end of the table.

"That sounds dangerous," adds her mom.

"But Mommy," Melody says, "you let me march in the protest at Fieldston's Clothing Store."

"That was organized," her mom says. "We didn't just show up there without thinking it through."

"And there were no bulldozers at Fieldston's," Melody's dad adds.

"Just because we move quickly doesn't mean we're

not organized," Yvonne says to her mother.

As Big Momma sets a bowl of potatoes on the table, she says, "There are other ways to raise your voices." She sounds worried, too.

Out of the corner of my eye, I see Yvonne and Melody exchange a look. Yvonne's jaw is set with determination. "I can bring the girls with me," she says. "I'll look out for them. I think it could be a good experience for them, to stand up for something they believe in."

Melody's parents look doubtful. I have to admit, standing in the way of a construction crew *does* sound dangerous. *What would my own parents think about that?* I wonder. My stomach flutters with nerves and homesickness.

Melody gives me that look again, the one that says, What do you think we should do?

To go to the demonstration, turn to page 122.

To raise your voices another way, turn to page 110.

ust then, the door jingles behind us. A white woman and her teenage daughter step into the shop. When the girl smiles at us, I smile back, but my cheek is quivering.

Sue, the waitress, comes back to the cash register. She puts the water pitcher down, grabs a couple of menus, and motions for the woman and her daughter to follow her.

The teenage girl points at me, Melody, and Yvonne. "They were here first," she says kindly.

The sour look on Sue's face says that the last thing she wants to do is seat us. Finally, she waves her hand toward a table in the way, way back. "There's a booth back there," she says.

Yvonne smiles politely. "We'll take these open seats right here, please," she says, stepping toward the counter.

Melody follows Yvonne toward the stools, her chin set in the same determined way as her sister's. I hurry along behind them, hoping my wobbly legs don't give out.

🎵 *Turn to page 115.*

efore the woman can say anything, Cousin Tish steps forward. "It looks like our girls have made friends," she says warmly, extending her hand. "I'm Tish Porter. It's very nice to meet you."

Time stands still as we all watch and wait. The white woman stares at Tish's outstretched hand. Then, finally, she extends her own.

I slowly release my breath. *Did I just help break down one of those walls that Yvonne was talking about?* I wonder. I think maybe, just maybe, I did.

Then I remember another neighbor girl, the dark-haired girl who moved in between Anika's house and mine. The last time I saw her, I was staring at her through the window, not waving or going out to say hello. *Did that make her feel bad?* I wonder. *Like I don't want her in my neighborhood?*

As we drive back to Melody's house, I realize something: It's time to go home. There's something I really, *really* want to do when I get there.

🎵 **Turn to page 124.**

*A*fter dinner, Melody and I sit on the front steps and make a plan.

"I'm kind of scared to go to the demonstration," I admit.

She looks relieved. "I am, too," she says. "But we *have* to help Auntie Josephine and Uncle Al. They're losing everything—even their piano. Can't we do something?"

I shrug. "Not unless we win a million dollars and can buy them a new piano."

Melody laughs. "Well, with a million dollars, we could buy them a whole new *building*."

"That's true," I say, propping my elbows on my knees. For some reason, an image of my dad pops into my mind. "That's it!" I say. "We can do a fund-raiser." I explain to Melody that my dad is a politician who raises money for his campaigns.

"Your dad is a politician?" she asks. She looks as starstruck as I was when I found out her brother is a Motown star.

"Yes," I say. "But the point is, we can fund-raise like he does. We can ask people to help Al and Josephine get a new piano."

Melody takes a deep breath and blows it out slowly. "That might not be so easy," she says. "My Junior Block Club wanted new swings at the playground. We wrote letters to the Parks Department, but it took a long time to get help." Melody shakes her head. "I don't know who to write to about a new piano for Uncle Al and Auntie Josephine."

"Hmm," I say, my hopes beginning to sink again. "If you want to raise money for a piano, you have to talk to people who care about music as much as we do."

That's when Melody gets a glint in her eye. "I know where to find people like that," she says. "My church."

"Yes!" I say. "Can we do a concert there or something?"

Melody chews her lip. "We can ask Miss Dorothy about it. Wait, there's already a concert on the church calendar. *Your* concert on Tuesday night."

Huh?

"The traveling youth choir, silly," she says.

Worry nibbles at my stomach. I'm not actually a part of that choir. "I'd much rather do a fund-raiser with *you*," I say.

Melody's face softens. "We could ask Miss Dorothy

if we can play something during the performance—like halfway through. Then we can talk to the congregation and ask them to donate money for the new piano."

I nod. "That could work!" Now my worry's gone and I'm feeling something else—pride. Melody and I put our heads together and came up with a good idea.

Dad would be proud of me, too, I think happily as I follow Melody inside.

🎵 *Turn to page 126.*

Is it a fire truck?" I ask, spinning around. The flashing lights are blinding.

"I think it's the police!" says Melody, her eyes wide.

Dwayne immediately pulls the car to the side of the street. His eyes in the rearview mirror look scared, but his mouth is set in a straight, hard line.

Did he do something wrong? I wonder. *Was he speeding?*

A police officer taps on the window next to Dwayne. Another officer appears on my side of the car.

Dwayne rolls the window all the way down, and the officer glances into the backseat at me and Melody. My stomach tightens, and I look away.

"This your car?" asks the officer hovering over Dwayne's window.

The other officer says, "How does a boy like you drive a car like this?"

What does he mean, "a boy like you"? I wonder. *Does he think Dwayne is too young to drive?*

"Answer me, boy," says the first officer. "This your car? Don't lie to me, now."

Then it hits me. I can tell by his voice that he thinks Dwayne *stole* this car.

"No, sir," Dwayne says politely, staring straight ahead. "I'm just borrowing the car from a friend."

The officer doesn't seem to believe him. "This friend got a name?" he asks. "How about if we take you down to the station and you can tell us more about this 'friend'?"

Melody's hand finds mine. I can feel her trembling.

Dwayne's voice is steady as he says, "This car belongs to Mr. James Hartman down at Hitsville, sir. Mr. Hartman is a producer."

The officer stares hard at Dwayne for what feels like an eternity. Then he says, "I'm gonna need you to step out of the car."

I freeze—I can't even breathe. *Is Dwayne going to get arrested?*

🎵 *Turn to page 131.*

The stool is cold and hard. I hold on tight to the counter to steady myself.

As the teenage girl and her mom sit down beside us, Sue grabs a pad and the pencil from behind her ear. "What can I get you?" she asks the girl's mother.

"Coffee for me, please," says the woman. "And two slices of cherry pie."

Sue jots that down. She turns toward the coffee pot, fills a cup, and places it on a saucer in front of the woman. But even after she serves the pie, Sue doesn't ask Yvonne, Melody, or me for our orders.

When Sue steps to the cash register, Yvonne says, "I'd like a cup of coffee, too, and a couple of sodas, please."

Sue doesn't look up. "We're out of coffee," she says curtly.

I can see the nearly full pot simmering behind the counter. Melody sees it, too. "There's coffee right there," she says to me, pointing.

Sue stares at us. The air feels cold and still, like just before a thunderstorm. Part of me wants to get off my stool and run away, before something bad happens. But I don't.

I remember Yvonne's words: *It's important to take a stand on things like this. Someone has to fight for what's right.*

"There's, um, plenty of coffee, isn't there?" I hear myself saying to Sue. My voice isn't loud. It sounds very far away. But Yvonne raises an eyebrow, as if she's impressed.

The white woman smiles at me, too. "Yes, the pot is definitely full," she says.

By the time Sue pours that cup of coffee for Yvonne, my palms are sweating. Melody and I get our sodas, too, and I swear, ice-cold soda *never* tasted so good.

Finally, I feel like a regular kid in a soda shop again. But I've learned something: Even girls like Melody and me can make a difference.

I guess sometimes taking a stand means being brave enough to sit down—to sit on a stool and wait to be served, just like everyone else.

🎵 *The End* 🎵

To read this story another way and see how different choices lead to a different ending, turn back to page 51.

*A*re you studying *already*?" Melody asks Lila. "School hasn't even started yet!"

We're standing at the kitchen counter at Melody's house, helping Yvonne and Melody's mom make bologna and cheese sandwiches. I'm adding lettuce and Melody is adding tomatoes. But Lila is hunched over the table in front of an open book.

"This happens to be my new American History book," says Lila. "And I'm not studying. I'm just *looking* at it."

"Focus on your own work, Melody," her mom scolds, handing her squares of wax paper. "Wrap those sandwiches tightly so that the tomato juice doesn't leak out."

Melody wipes her hands on a paper napkin. "The tomatoes are definitely juicy," she says, popping a slice into her mouth. "I grew them myself."

"Really?" I say.

"Sure," she says. "And the lettuce. My garden is out back."

"Those vegetables are going to feed a bunch of volunteers today, Dee-Dee," says Yvonne. "You should feel good about that." She doesn't sound upset about the soda shop anymore.

Melody nods proudly. Then she spots Lila sniffing the pages of her new book. "I think Lila wants to eat her *book* instead of a bologna sandwich," she jokes.

Lila laughs sheepishly. "I can't help it!" she says. "I love the smell of books."

I laugh, too. I know just how she feels.

"Volunteers could have used more books like that when they were teaching at Freedom Schools down in Mississippi this summer," says Yvonne. "They didn't have a lot of great materials to work with."

"Well, that's been true even here in Detroit," adds Melody's mom. "We're finally getting materials in my classroom that teach about black history—and that show the miseries of slavery instead of painting a pretty picture of it. But we've sure waited a long time for them."

As I wrap my last sandwich in wax paper, I try to imagine that. In fourth grade, we spent the whole month of February learning about black history. I got an A on my report about Frederick Douglass, who escaped from slavery and became a great writer and leader. What if I'd never learned about him? Or Harriet Tubman? Or the Underground Railroad? A whole

chunk of history would just be . . . *missing.*

A bark at the back door makes us all jump. It's Bo waiting to be let out.

"I'll take him," says Lila, reaching for the dog's leash.

I wash my hands and then take a seat at the table. While I wait for Melody to finish, I flip through Lila's new book. *What will it say about Frederick Douglass?* I wonder. I page to the index and slide my finger down the Ds. But Frederick Douglass isn't listed. *Huh.*

I search the Ts next for Harriet Tubman. Nothing. My cheeks start to burn.

When Lila comes back inside, I close the book—too quickly.

"What is it?" she asks. "What did you see?"

I don't know how to tell her that it's not what I saw. It's what I *didn't* see.

 *Turn to page 128.*

*A*s soon as we climb into Dwayne's old car to head home, Melody taps on the back of his seat. "Tell us, Dwayne!" she says. "What do you need my help with?"

Dwayne spins around and rests his arm on the seat. "Okay, check this out," he says. "I'm cutting another record—another single."

"Really?" says Melody. "Two records in one summer? Wow . . . The Three Ravens must be hitting it big!"

Dwayne cuts her off. "Not The Three Ravens," he says. "This one I'm doing on my own. I know this guy who owns a small studio, and he owes me a favor, so . . . I'm going to record some of my own stuff Monday night."

Melody's mouth hangs open. "You're leaving The Three Ravens?" she says.

"No," says Dwayne quickly. "It's nothing like that. I just want to try a solo song. But Artie and Phil don't know yet, so . . ."

Melody pinches her thumb and finger together and slides them across her lips, as if zipping her mouth closed.

Dwayne's face softens. "Thanks, Dee-Dee. Now are

you going to help your brother-man rehearse?"

She nods. "We both can," she says, grinning at me. "Tomorrow. At Big Momma's. Right?"

"Right," I say, remembering the last time we played music together there. I can't wait!

🎵 *Turn to page 136.*

By nighttime, Melody and I have made a big decision. We're going to the demonstration tomorrow, but I'm still nervous—especially when Melody tells me why Yvonne's wrist is in a cast. "She broke it when she got arrested," she explains.

"Arrested? When? Why?" I say, the questions tumbling out of my mouth.

"In Mississippi. She went down with other college students to help black people register to vote and to teach school to kids. Some people in the area—some white people—weren't too happy about that. Yvonne was just talking to some black folks and she got arrested for disturbing the peace. A police officer pulled her off their porch, and that's when she tripped and hurt herself."

I can't believe what I'm hearing. Yvonne seems even braver now, but I feel more scared than ever. *Will we get arrested tomorrow, too?* I want to ask. *Or hurt?* But I don't want to disappoint Melody, and I know that Al and Josephine need our help—no matter what.

Even though tomorrow is really important, there's something I have to admit to Melody. It's just too big to keep inside. "I'm kind of homesick," I tell her. "I think

I need to go home tomorrow. After the demonstration, I mean."

Melody looks surprised. "Don't you have to wait for the choir bus?" she asks.

I shake my head. "No, I can get home on my own," I say honestly. "I haven't left yet because it's been really fun to stay with you and your family. But now I want to see my own family."

Melody's face falls, but she squeezes my hand. I know she understands.

"I'm glad you'll be at the demonstration in the morning," she says. "I wouldn't want to be there without you."

🎵 *Turn to page 139.*

Turn to page 139.

aying good-bye to Melody is hard, but when I'm back in that church basement, I can't wait to sit at the piano and play my way home. I close my eyes, remembering the melody for "Lift Every Voice and Sing." *I found a new way to lift my voice today*, I realize, remembering the moment when I invited Val's neighbor to swing with us.

As soon as I'm back in my bedroom, I grab my phone. It *dings* in my hand—a text from Anika. I write back immediately: *Meet me outside.* Then I run to Mom's office.

"Can I go outside and play?" I ask.

Mom looks surprised. She nods but then asks, "What about practicing the piano?"

I grin. "There's something more important that I've got to do."

As I step outside, I hear voices. My new neighbor is still playing Frisbee with her brother. As I round the corner of the house, she smiles shyly.

I cross the grass to introduce myself, and I see Anika hurrying down her front steps toward us, too. Then this warm feeling spreads through me like a sip of hot cocoa. I just *know* that the three of us are going to

get along well, kind of like I knew that Melody and I would.

For a moment, I miss Melody. But in some ways, it feels like she's still with me, helping me break down walls and make a difference—right here at home.

🎵 *The End* 🎵

To read this story another way and see how different choices lead to a different ending, turn back to page 13.

O n Monday, we call Miss Dorothy, who thinks the fund-raiser is a great idea. Now there's only one thing left to do: choose a song to play.

"We don't have a lot of time to practice," says Melody. "Maybe we should play a song we already know."

"Right," I say. "What do we both know?"

We're sitting on Big Momma's couch when it comes to us, just as it did on Saturday night. "'His Eye Is on the Sparrow,'" we say together.

"Yes!" says Melody, clapping her hands together.

"It's perfect," I say, "because we heard it first at the performance hall. Should we practice it now?"

We sit together at Big Momma's piano, and I'm thrilled to see that my fingers still remember the notes. Melody knows every word of the song, too, because her youth choir sang it.

We practice the song several times, polishing it until it's perfect. Melody brushes her hands together as we finish one last time. "This sounds *good*!"

That's when it strikes me: I'm not going to *look* all that good Tuesday night. I should dress up for the concert, but I don't have anything fancy to wear.

*n*ow everyone's staring at me—not just Lila, but Melody, Yvonne, and their mom, too. "What's wrong?" Melody asks.

I feel the same pressure I did when we were standing outside Sam's Soda Shop. I'd chickened out then—I was too scared to go inside. *Are you going to chicken out again now?* I ask myself.

I swallow the lump in my throat and point toward the book. "There's, um, some really important stuff missing in here." I tell them that I can't find anything about Frederick Douglass or Harriet Tubman.

"Really?" says Yvonne, crossing the floor. As she flips through the book, I can tell she's getting angry.

"When was it printed?" asks Melody's mom.

Yvonne turns to the first few pages. "In 1959," she says. "Just five years ago. But I can't even find a picture of a black person in here." Despite her injured wrist, she flips through the pages so fast, I'm afraid she's going to rip one.

Lila puts her hand on Yvonne's and says, "Wait, I just saw one!" But when Yvonne turns back a page or two, Lila's face crumples. "Oh," she says. "It's a picture of a slave."

"So the only black people featured in this book are slaves," says Yvonne, shaking her head.

Lila's brow furrows. "No black scientists or inventors? What about George Washington Carver?" She checks the index again and then slumps back in her chair. "I thought I was going to a good school!"

Her mom squeezes her shoulders. "In a lot of ways, it *is* a good school. But it's a mostly white school, so some changes are going to be slower in coming."

Lila falls silent, but Melody stirs beside her. "You can change things, Lila," she says. "You can write letters to your school—like the Junior Block Club did when we wanted to make the playground better. Remember how we wrote to the Parks Department?"

Lila nods, and I can see her spark return.

"That's a good idea, Melody," Mrs. Ellison says.

"I'll help you write letters," Melody promises Lila. "We'll tell your school how books like this make us feel, and we'll ask them to buy new books."

"New books that teach about *all* the famous black scientists," adds Lila. "Like Carver, Charles Drew, Lewis Latimer . . . " She counts them off on her fingers.

"Can I help, too?" I ask. I want to help make things

better for Lila—and for all the students at her school.

Lila grins and hugs me and Melody at the same time.

"That's the spirit," says Yvonne, clapping her hands together.

♫ *Turn to page 133.*

Dwayne opens the door and steps onto the sidewalk. That's when Melody tugs on my hand and darts out the door, too. "We'll go get Mr. Hartman!" she says to the officers. "We'll go get him right now."

I trip out of the car after her, our hands still connected.

"Melody, no!" says Dwayne. "You stay put."

But the officer holds Dwayne back. "Let 'em go," says the officer. "I want to hear what this Mr. Hartman has to say."

Melody takes off down the street and I race behind her, my eyes fixed on her bouncing braids. I don't look over my shoulder. I'm afraid I'll see the officers arresting Dwayne.

When we reach the studio, we burst through the front doors. Melody calls out the producer's name. "Mr. Hartman!"

Artie pokes his head out of a room. "Melody, what—?" he starts to say.

But a man in a suit comes down the hall from the other direction. "I'm Mr. Hartman," he says, his brow furrowed. "What's wrong?"

Melody tells him all in one breath. She finishes

with, "They're going to arrest Dwayne!"

Mr. Hartman's eyes widen, and he runs out the door ahead of us. Artie goes, too.

"But why?" I ask Melody as we take the steps two at a time. "Why do they think Dwayne stole the car?"

"Because," she says, her eyes welling up with tears. "Because he's black, and they don't think a black person could own a car like that." Then she sets her jaw and takes off down the street again.

We can't catch up with Artie and Mr. Hartman, but we try. *Will Dwayne still be there when we get to the car?* I wonder. *Or will he be on his way to jail?*

🎵 *Turn to page 144.*

On Monday afternoon, we're back at the church with the Student Walk to Freedom Club. The pile of envelopes on the table makes me proud.

"I sure hope this works," says Melody, licking the last envelope and sealing it shut.

"Me, too," I say.

Yvonne gives a big thank-you to the volunteers. "We did our part today to help black students get a good education," she says proudly. "They need to learn about leaders in black history. That's how they begin to believe that they can become leaders, too."

I let those words sink in. *I kind of already feel like a leader*, I realize. Dad would be proud of me for getting involved—for telling Melody's family what I found in that book instead of pretending I didn't see. Mom would be proud, too.

That's when it hits me how much I miss my parents. It's time to go home.

After everyone leaves the community room, I break the news to Melody. She's sad, but I think she feels just as good as I do about everything we did together. "Do you want me to wait here with you?" she asks sweetly. She thinks my parents are coming to pick me up.

"No," I tell her. "That'll just make me more sad." It's true. Leaving my new friend is hard. I have to make my good-bye quick—like ripping off a bandage.

So after she follows Yvonne up the stairs, I sit down at the piano. I hum the melody for "Lift Every Voice," and then I start to play.

This time, the voices that swell up around me belong to the people I've met on my journey: Melody's pure, sweet voice and Big Momma's low, powerful voice. If I listen hard, I can even hear Lila and Yvonne, doing their sister-thing.

I know I'm home when I hear the *ding* of my phone. It's probably Anika, but I don't have time to answer right now. Instead, I fling open my bedroom door and race down the hall.

I can't wait to see Mom again, to tell her that I'm proud of her. I'm proud that she's a principal and that she fights to make sure kids get a good education.

And when Dad gets home, maybe I'll ask him more about his job, too. Now that I know that girls like Melody and me can make a difference, it makes me wonder, *What can I do here in my own hometown?*

I laugh, imagining how excited my dad will be to

hear me ask that. He'll have plenty of ideas for me, but I know now that I'll have a few good ideas of my *own*, too.

The End

To read this story another way and see how different choices lead to a different ending, turn back to page 80.

*O*n Sunday afternoon, we watch Melody's grandparents pull out of the driveway.

"They're driving to Canada?" I ask, trying to figure out how they can drive to another *country* just for the day.

"The Emancipation Celebration festival is across the river in Windsor, Ontario," Melody explains. "It only takes a half hour or so to get there." She sighs as she shuts the door. "Part of me wishes we could have gone with them, but Dwayne needs our help."

She's right. When Dwayne arrives, he looks anxious. He shakes out his arms and legs. "I've got the jitters," he says.

"You?" says Melody. "You *never* get nervous!"

Dwayne shrugs. "What can I say?" he says. "Guess I got used to having Artie and Phil standing there beside me."

"Well, we'll be Artie and Phil today," Melody says. "I mean"—she makes her voice as deep as it'll go—"we'll be Artie and Phil today."

Dwayne laughs and pulls one of her pigtails. "Thanks, Dee-Dee. I'll take you up on that."

He sits at the piano and starts playing something

slow and sweet. When he hits a sour note, he shakes out his hands again. "I'm so jazzed right now, I can't even remember the notes. I'll be right back—I need my music."

He darts out the front door, and we hear a car door slam. Then he's back with a sheet of music in his hands. It's handwritten and messy, but when Dwayne sits back down at the piano, the music pours out of his fingertips.

Melody and I cheer like crazy when he's done. "I can't believe you wrote that!" I tell him.

"And you played it perfectly," adds Melody. "You're ready!"

Dwayne shakes his head. "Thanks," he says. "But I've gotta practice it away from the piano. The house band at the studio will play for me so I can focus on my voice." He clears his throat and sings a few bars.

"Wait," says Melody. "We can be your band. It'll feel more real that way."

She points me toward the piano, where Dwayne's handwritten music is still set up. I shrug. Why not? As long as I can read it, I should be able to play it.

As I sit at the piano, Melody disappears into the

kitchen—and comes back out with a pan and a wooden spoon. Dwayne laughs. "Just like the old days, eh, little sis?" he says. "You're the best saucepan drummer I know."

Melody turns the pan upside down, tapping the bottom with the wooden spoon. It *does* sound like a drum, especially when I play piano and Dwayne sings along.

When we finish, Dwayne doesn't seem so nervous anymore. "I've got my house band right here," he says. "What more does a guy need? Except maybe a microphone."

Melody and I look at each other and grin. She gets to the fruit bowl first and tosses Dwayne a banana.

He stares at the fruit and then laughs. "Looks like I'm gonna have to change the name of my band after today," he says. "Dwayne and the Banana Splits." Then he peels the banana and takes a big bite.

♫ *Turn to page 145.*

*m*onday morning comes way too quickly. Before I know it, Yvonne is standing in Big Momma's living room. Her eyes are lit up, like she's been awake for hours. Now that I know how Yvonne's wrist got hurt, I'm even more impressed with her courage. No wonder she doesn't seem nervous about today.

"Are you girls ready?" Yvonne asks.

"Ready," says Melody. "Except we have to tell Big Momma we're leaving—and I know she's going to worry." She calls upstairs, but there's no response.

Yvonne and I follow Melody into the kitchen, where we find a note on the counter. It reads:

Went to visit a friend. Help yourself to breakfast, and I'll be back soon.—Big Momma

"She's already gone!" says Melody with a loud sigh of relief. "Good. Now no one will be worried about us going to the demonstration."

Except me, I think. But there's no turning back now.

We set out for 12th Street, Yvonne in the lead. The distance feels farther on foot than it did in Miss Dorothy's car last night. And Yvonne is walking so fast, Melody and I can barely keep up.

"Slow down, Vonnie," Melody cries.

But Yvonne keeps going. "We don't want to be late," she calls over her shoulder.

And then it occurs to me: *What if the construction crew is already there? What if the demolition has started?*

My fast walk turns into a run.

🎝 ***Turn to page 148.***

It's Tuesday evening—"Matching Tuesday," Melody calls it. I'm sitting on a church bench wearing pink hair ribbons, and Melody is, too. Her dress has pink flowers on it, and the one that Lila loaned to me is solid pink. But the folds of my skirt are gathered with a bow at the waist, just like Melody's.

"My friend Sharon and I do Matching Mondays at school," she told me this afternoon when we were standing in front of her closet. "But you and I'll do a Matching Tuesday, okay?"

Definitely okay, I think. For the first time in my life, I feel like I have a sister. I wish I could take her home with me!

The youth choir is just finishing the first half of their performance. I told Melody I was too nervous about our song to sing with the choir, which is true. Butterflies flit through my chest.

"Thank you to the Second Baptist Youth Choir for visiting us here in Detroit," says Miss Dorothy, standing at the microphone. "Thank you for lifting your beautiful voices for us." She claps for the choir, and the congregation joins in.

Then she says, "Before the youth choir concludes

their performance, we have two more performers with a special request. Girls, are you ready?"

My knees wobble as I follow Melody to the front of the church. As I sit down on the piano bench, she steps to the microphone. Her voice shakes as she introduces us. But she doesn't let her nerves stop her from doing what's right.

"There's a performance hall on 12th Street that some of you might know," she says, describing Al and Josephine's place.

Most of the people in the congregation nod their heads, and several people even clap.

"Well, the city is supposed to start tearing it down this week," says Melody sadly.

Low murmurs ripple through the congregation.

"The owners of the hall, Al and Josephine Moore, lost everything—their home, their business, and even their piano. They have to start all over," says Melody. "My friend and I want to raise money to buy a new piano so that they can keep playing music. Will you help us?" Applause spreads like a wave across the congregation.

Melody grins at me. Then she says, "We're going

to play a song that reminds us all that we're not alone. Then we'll pass the collection plates, in case you want to donate money for the new piano. Thank you."

As Melody bows her head, there are more cheers and claps. And then it's time to begin.

Turn to page 154.

*L*ook!" Melody pants. She points down the street at the red Mustang, still parked along the curb with the officers standing beside it. Dwayne must be inside the car. Phew!

Mr. Hartman is gesturing with his hands, talking to the officers. Artie stands off to the side, like he's afraid to get too close. Then Mr. Hartman ducks his head into the car and pops back out with an envelope.

"The registration is right here," he says, handing it to an officer. He pulls out his wallet and offers his driver's license, too.

The officers study the registration, as if they think it's fake. But they finally nod at Mr. Hartman and hand back the paperwork.

I wait until they're back in their police car and pulling away from the curb. Then I let out my breath. I feel sick to my stomach.

Melody's face is twisted with emotion. "Dwayne!" she calls, rushing to the door of the Mustang.

🎵 *Turn to page 152.*

On Monday night, Dwayne drives us to the recording studio, which is in the basement of a record shop. As soon as I step out of the car, I hear music.

"Where's that coming from?" asks Melody.

"The studio. That's a record being made," Dwayne says. "The sound gets piped out through speakers right onto the sidewalk. It's my voice you'll be hearing next." He smiles nervously.

We wait in the record shop for the recording to finish. Dwayne paces the aisles, but Melody and I flip through albums. I've never seen so many records— rows and rows of the flat, square covers. Grammy had a collection, but hers all fit into one little cupboard.

Then Melody races over to a section of small records tucked into paper sleeves. She searches through them and pulls out a shiny black disc with a bright blue label. I see the word "Motown" written across the top.

"Have you heard this one?" she asks with a smile.

I squint to read the label: *Move On Up. The Three Ravens.* "Is this Dwayne's record?" I squeal. "Is your voice on here, too, Melody?"

She nods, grinning.

I wish I could listen to the record right now. But when a few guys with instrument cases come up from the basement, Dwayne waves us toward the stairs. "Let's go, girls," he says. "We're up."

When we get downstairs, a man wearing headphones nods at Dwayne. Then he glances behind us. "Where's your band?" he asks.

"It's just me, Mac," says Dwayne. "It's a solo recording, remember?"

Mac says, "No, I mean your musicians."

"You don't have a house band?" Dwayne asks.

Mac snorts. "This ain't Motown, brother. We can't afford to keep musicians on the payroll."

Dwayne sighs. "I can play the piano, too," he says, shaking out his hands. "I've just been so focused on the vocals."

Mac frowns. "You want to do this another day, Dwayne? I mean, if you're not ready . . ."

Dwayne's shoulders sag. He looks at the clock, as if he can't stand to let another second go by before doing this thing.

"We can be your band," Melody pipes up. "Just like we practiced."

My stomach drops. Practicing in someone's living room is one thing. Playing in a studio for a recording that will be heard by thousands of people . . . that's totally different!

🎵 *Turn to page 156.*

*W*hen we're a block away from the performance hall, we see a yellow crane and lots of men wearing white hard hats. "Oh, no," groans Melody. "Are we too late?"

"No," says Yvonne. "I don't think they've started yet. But let's hurry."

Then we see something else: a crowd of people, mostly teenagers, gathered in front of the building. Melody stops short, and I plow into the back of her, making her fall forward.

"Sorry," I say, reaching out to steady her. "What's wrong?"

She points. It's Josephine, standing tall and proud among the crowd. And next to her? Big Momma. She sees us at the same moment, and she opens her arms wide.

Big Momma has tears in her eyes when we reach her. "I couldn't stay away either, baby chicks," she says. "Some things are just worth fighting for."

I feel safe wrapped up in Big Momma's hug, until I hear sirens. A nervous energy runs through the crowd of protesters, and Big Momma pulls Melody and me even closer.

A construction crew manager jogs over to meet the police officers as they climb out of a squad car. They talk for a moment, and then the police officers walk toward us. Melody's hand slips into mine. I squeeze it tight.

Yvonne doesn't shrink back. She steps forward to meet the officers. "We're staging a peaceful protest," she says in a clear, brave voice.

Isn't she afraid she'll be arrested again? I wonder.

"Peaceful or not, miss," says the first officer, "you're standing in the way of city business. We need you to clear out—now."

When no one moves, the second officer strokes his mustache. "Go on home now," he says. "You're just a bunch of kids. This doesn't involve you."

He sounds like he's trying to be nice, but his words sting. *We may be kids,* I think, *but we **are** involved. We know what matters. This performance hall matters. Music matters.*

Yvonne reaches out her right hand to the boy next to her. Others clasp hands, too, until they form a wall between the police and the building behind them.

I reach for Melody's hand, and then Big Momma's.

None of the volunteers flinch or move out of the way, not even when the first officer starts talking about arresting us. "Anyone who refuses to leave will be taken downtown," he says.

I can tell that the officer with the mustache doesn't want that. "Let's all just go on home now," he tries again.

I look up at Big Momma. "Are they really going to arrest us all?" I whisper. She pulls me toward her. Melody's eyes widen, too.

"Don't be scared," Big Momma says. "You know what we're gonna do? We're gonna sing. Sing with love in our hearts and a good feeling in our souls." With that, Big Momma's low, powerful voice begins.

> *We shall not,*
> *We shall not be moved.*

Josephine joins in right away. Then Melody is singing, too, and her sweet, high voice is strong.

> *Just like a tree that's standing by the water,*
> *We shall not be moved.*

As the others around us begin to sing, something happens. It's like someone tipped a bucket of warm water inside me, and it fills me with such a good feeling that I can't help it. I start singing, too.

My voice isn't as deep and strong as Big Momma's. It's not as pure and sweet as Melody's. But it's all I've got, and I sing with everything I have in me.

We keep singing, and we sing for a long time. When one of the protesters starts a song I don't know, I hum along until the words are familiar. That warm-water feeling stays with me.

The construction crew stands and watches while their manager talks to the police. I'm still singing when a police van appears. All of a sudden, the officers lead a group of protesters toward the van. One of them is Yvonne!

🎵 *Turn to page 157.*

*A*re you sure you're okay?" Melody asks Dwayne.

"I'm fine, Dee-Dee," he says. "It's not the first time I've been stopped by the police, and it's probably not gonna be the last." He's in the passenger seat now next to Mr. Hartman, who is driving us back to the studio.

Artie sits between me and Melody. "They pull over black guys all the time," he says. "For no good reason."

Mr. Hartman sighs. "I think we need more black officers on the police force," he says. "If more of them looked like you and me, they wouldn't be looking at us as if we were criminals."

Dwayne's face is set in stone. He doesn't look scared anymore, but he doesn't look mad either. He's just staring straight ahead.

I can still hear the way he talked to that police officer, calling him "sir." But the police officer called *him* "boy." Grammy always told me that people who act with respect will be treated with respect. That sure didn't happen tonight.

"It's not fair," I say to Melody. Dwayne overhears.

"Lots of things aren't fair," he says. "That's how it's always been and how it's always gonna be." Suddenly,

Dwayne grins. "I'm just gonna keep playing my music. Someday, I'll make enough money to buy a Mustang of my own." He winks at Melody and adds, "With papers to prove it!"

I can't believe he's not angry anymore! *Dwayne may not be a famous singer yet,* I think to myself, *but he's kind of already a star. He treats himself and other people with respect.*

Those officers may not have respected him back, but I sure do. So maybe Grammy was right after all.

I think of Zoey Gatz, sticking out her tongue or strutting down the red carpet. Sure, she has lots of money, but she doesn't act like she respects herself—or anyone else. Somehow, she seems kind of silly to me now.

Maybe when I get home, I'll take down my Zoey Gatz posters and put up something new. There are plenty of talented people to choose from, now that I know where—and when—to look for them.

🎵 *The End* 🎵

To read this story another way and see how different choices lead to a different ending, turn back to page 13.

(m)y heart races as I play those first few notes, almost as if I'm playing in front of judges at a piano recital. But something's different. *You're not alone,* I remind myself. *Melody is right here beside you.*

There's something else, too: My heart feels so full, it almost hurts. Tonight, I'm definitely playing with *passion,* as Ms. Stricker would say. How could I not? Melody and I are performing for something that matters, *really* matters.

Melody's voice rises up to meet the rafters. Wow! She sounds even better than she did at Big Momma's. And she doesn't look scared anymore.

> *I sing because I'm happy,*
> *I sing because I'm free*

People in the audience sing, too, raising their hands and their voices upward.

> *For His eye is on the sparrow,*
> *And I know He watches me.*

I feel like I'm right back at the performance hall in the midst of a crowd that is moved by the music.

As Melody sings the last few words, someone nudges me. It's Miss Dorothy, holding out a wooden collection plate. "Let's pass the plates while that gorgeous music is still ringing in their ears," she says, winking at me.

Melody takes a plate, too, and we stand on opposite ends of the benches, passing the plates back and forth along the rows of people. Every time the plate comes back to me, I try not to count how much money is in it. Even if there's not enough for a new piano, I hope there's enough to let Al and Josephine know that people care.

As we hand the full plates to Miss Dorothy at the back of the church, Melody and I lock eyes and smile.

"Psst . . ." says someone from the hallway. It's Big Momma. "C'mon, chicks," she says, waving us out into the hall. "I have a surprise for you."

🎵 *Turn to page 160.*

I feel frozen, like I did at Hitsville. Playing key-board for Dwayne's recording feels even scarier, though. I can't *pretend* to play, like I pretended to sing. And I can't mess up!

Mac frowns at Melody and me like we're little kids.

"They can do it," Dwayne says. "They're good."

I stand taller then. *Dwayne believes in us*, I think. *He needs us.*

Dwayne hands me the sheet music, and for a moment, all those notes blur together. But when Melody picks up a tambourine from the instrument rack, the jingle clears my head.

Pretend there's no one else in the room, I tell myself. *It's just me, Dwayne, and Melody.* At Dwayne's cue, I start to play. And I do pretty well. We only have to record the song twice! It's like Dwayne and the Banana Splits have been playing together forever. And then, before I know it, it's over.

I follow Dwayne and Melody back upstairs into the record shop. There, we stop short. A crowd of people is gathered outside the front window. What's going on?

🎵 **Turn to page 159.**

*V*onnie!" squeals Melody, lunging forward.

"She's okay, baby," Big Momma soothes. "She's going to be all right."

But Melody breaks free and races after her sister.

"Melody!" Big Momma cries, pushing through the crowd after her. "Melody Elizabeth Ellison!"

I try to follow, but there are too many people! Their hands are locked together, holding me back. When I finally break free, I see a police officer coming my way. Is he going to arrest me? I run the other way— toward the performance hall. Then I hear my name. I spin around wildly, trying to find Melody. Where is she?

She's across the street, with Big Momma by her side. Melody is waving me toward her, but I can't get there. The river of people is too wide to cross.

I stumble into someone. It's Josephine.

"It's okay, sweetie," she says soothingly. "We'll get you to Melody." She takes my hand and starts to push her way through the crowd. But there's only one place I want to go right now: *home.*

I tug back on Josephine's hand. "Can you do something for me?" I ask her.

"Anything, baby," she says, leaning close.

"Please tell Melody I had to go home," I say. "She knows"—my voice catches a little—"she knows I miss my family."

Josephine hesitates. "All right, but let me take you," she says. "I'll take you home."

I shake my head. "I can get there," I say. "It's close."

And it is, if I can just get to a piano. Then I remember the old piano inside the performance hall. Is it safe? I scan the crowd, looking for the construction crew. "Miss Josephine, look," I say, barely breathing.

She follows my gaze and sees the construction workers heading toward their trucks.

"Are they leaving?" I ask.

Josephine shakes her head. "They're just taking a coffee break, I think," she says. "They have to wait for the police to clear the crowd, which will take a while."

That's all I need to hear. I hug Josephine, and then as she makes her way across the crowded street, I go the other way—toward the door of the performance hall. When I'm sure no one is looking, I duck inside.

🎵 *Turn to page 162.*

hat are they here for?" asks Melody, pointing toward the crowd of people outside.

The store clerk says, "They're waiting for more music. They're loving your sound."

Wow. The people out there liked our music. They want to hear more!

Melody bites her lip, trying not to smile too wide. But Dwayne steps into the middle of the crowd like a superstar, holding his head high.

As I follow him, I make a plan. When I get back home, I'll search online for his record. *Will I be able to find it?* I wonder. *And if I do, will I hear my own keyboard playing?*

I may never be a superstar myself, but now I'm thinking that's okay. As I walk beside Dwayne, I'm feeling pretty proud of what we just did. I guess you don't always have to be the star to shine.

🎵 *The End* 🎵

To read this story another way and see how different choices lead to a different ending, turn back to page 85.

I instantly recognize the couple standing next to Big Momma. It's Al and Josephine! Were they here all along?

"Girls, that was really something special," says Josephine, her eyes glistening. "Thank you from the bottom of my heart."

So they *did* hear the performance!

Al adds, "If we ever open another hall, I hope you'll consider performing. You could be the next big act."

"I like the sound of that," says Melody.

I do, too. I'm proud that I could use my talents to help Al and Josephine. And I've never had so much fun creating music as I've had these last few days with Melody. I don't want to say good-bye to her, but I know it's almost time.

After the youth choir finishes, I go to the restroom to change out of Lila's fancy dress and into my own clothes. Then I hurry back out to Melody and Big Momma.

"Your voice was so beautiful tonight," I tell Melody.

"Thanks," is the only word she can get out. She looks as if she's going to cry.

"Melody sang like an angel," Big Momma agrees,

rubbing Melody's back. Then she reaches for my hands and says, "But your hands are *your* strength, baby, your light. You know that, right? You have to let your own light shine."

Big Momma won't let go—not until I nod and show her that I understand. Then she says, "Good. Now you two chicks say your good-byes." As she steps away, I see that she's fighting tears, too.

I pull Melody into a hug. All I can say to her is, "Thank you. I'll never forget you." She still smells like roses, left over from one of Big Momma's embraces. I breathe in the scent, hoping I'll remember it always, and then I let go.

My throat is tight as I hurry downstairs toward the community room. A few of the youth choir members are leaving, carrying their black-and-white gowns on hangers.

When the room is empty, I sit down. Then I quietly, but quickly, play the song—the song that will take me home.

🎵 *Turn to page 163.*

I t's so dark in here! As my eyes adjust, I see the shadowy stage and the hulking piano at the back of the room. I hurry down the aisle and crawl up onto the stage. There's no piano bench to sit on, but that's okay. I lean forward over the keys.

I start to play, but my hands are shaking. I fumble and start over.

I do better the second time, but halfway through, I hear the deep voice of a police officer. "Who's in here?" he calls. The glare of a flashlight streaks across the room.

Don't stop, I tell myself. *Keep playing!*

♪ *Turn to page 164.*

Back in my bedroom, I soak up the silence. Then the *ding* of my phone jolts me into action. It's a text from Anika:

What happened???

She's responding to my text, the one I sent her a couple of minutes ago—minutes that feel like days.

I scroll up to my text: *You won't believe what happened today.*

Will she believe it? I don't know. So I just tell her the most important part:

Mom said there's no money for guitars in music class, but I came up with the BEST idea for a fund-raiser. We're going to have a concert!

I didn't even know I had the idea until it poured out of my fingertips into the text. But now, I can't wait to talk to Mom about it. Maybe Ms. Stricker can help, too. Maybe we can raise money at the piano recital!

I drop the phone on my bed and race out the bedroom door. "Mom!"

🎵 *The End* 🎵

To read this story another way and see how different choices lead to a different ending, turn back to page 38.

don't stop. I play as if my life depended on it.

And when I reach the end of the song, something shines brightly into my eyes. The flashlight? No. It's afternoon sunlight pouring through my bedroom window. I'm home. I'm home!

I push away from my keyboard, wanting to run to my mom. But when I fling open my bedroom door, Mom's already there. I throw myself into her arms.

"Honey, what is it?" she asks, stroking my hair.

"I . . . just missed you," I say, pressing my face against her shoulder.

She squeezes me tight and says, "I heard you playing."

Uh-oh.

"That song . . ." she says. "You played with so much passion, so much feeling. Your grandma would have loved it."

"I know." I swallow hard and say, "I really miss Grammy."

Mom says, "Me, too. But when you play that song, I feel like Grammy's still here with us. I hope you'll keep playing music like that. Will you?"

"I will," I say, my voice cracking. I only wish Al and

Josephine could keep playing, too—that they could keep their business. Will Melody and her family keep fighting for it?

Then I remember something. "Mom?" I say. "About the guitars. I don't think we should give up so easily. Music is . . . well, it's worth fighting for."

Mom smiles. "I feel the same way. I'll keep pushing for the music program, sweetie."

"Me, too, Mom. I'll help," I promise her. I don't know how yet, but I do know one thing: I've found my passion.

Cool relief washes over me. And when Mom asks if I want to come read in her office now, I'm ready.

"Thank you, Melody," I whisper. I take one last look at my keyboard and then follow Mom down the hall.

🎵 *The End* 🎵

To read this story another way and see how different choices lead to a different ending, turn back to page 107.

ABOUT Melody's Time

When Melody was growing up in the 1960s, the civil rights movement had many well-known leaders. People like Dr. Martin Luther King Jr., Rosa Parks, Ella Baker, and John Lewis took action against segregation and discrimination. There were also thousands of ordinary citizens who fought for equality. Many of them were young adults, high school students, and children Melody's age and younger.

Six-year-old Ruby Bridges bravely attended an all-white school in Louisiana in 1960. She was the first black child to go to a white school in the South, and most of the white parents did not want her there. Crowds gathered in front of the building yelling insults and throwing things at her. One woman even threatened to poison Ruby! But Ruby didn't back down—and she didn't miss a single day of first grade. Her courage and strength helped pave the way for school integration so that children of all races could learn together.

This same kind of courage and strength filled the streets of Birmingham, Alabama, in May 1963. When Dr. King and other civil rights organizers planned to protest segregation, many of Birmingham's black citizens were afraid to participate. They worried that their white employers would fire them for joining the marches. Many couldn't afford to go without pay if they got arrested and missed work. So the children of Birmingham stepped in.

Audrey Faye Hendricks, a nine-year-old, was one of them. On the morning of May 2, Audrey left school and joined 800 other children from all over the city in a peaceful protest. She was arrested and spent seven days in jail. "I wasn't nervous or scared," Audrey said about marching. After a week in jail, she knew her courage and strength had made a difference. "I felt like I was helping to gain what we were trying to get, and that was freedom."

Many of the event's organizers were worried about letting kids participate. No one wanted children to get hurt. Despite their concerns, leaders let the kids march in what became known as "the Children's Crusade." The kids' spirits were high. They laughed and sang as they headed to City Hall, and crowds gathered to cheer on the young protesters.

The next day, more than 1,500 kids showed up to protest. But the positive mood quickly changed when the police blasted the marchers with fire hoses, knocking the children off their feet. Police then used dogs to attack the protesters. Images of the event were in the papers and on the news. The use of violence captured national headlines, and people were shocked.

The Children's Crusade was an important turning point in the civil rights movement. It made people pay attention to the inequalities black people faced. The extraordinary role young people played in the event inspired courage and strength in girls like Melody who went on to make a difference in their own communities.

Read more of MELODY'S stories,

available from booksellers and at *americangirl.com*

♪ *Classics* ♪

Melody's classic series, now in two volumes:

Volume 1:
No Ordinary Sound

Melody can't wait to sing her first solo at church. She spends the summer practicing the perfect song—and helping her brother become a Motown singer. When an unimaginable tragedy leaves her silent, Melody has to find her voice.

Volume 2:
Never Stop Singing

Now that her brother is singing for Motown, Melody gets to visit a real recording studio. She also starts a children's block club. Melody is determined to help her neighborhood bloom—and make her community stronger.

♪ *Journey in Time* ♪

Travel back in time—and spend a few days with Melody!

Music in My Heart

Step into Melody's world of the 1960s! Volunteer with a civil rights group, join a demonstration, or use your voice to sing backup for a Motown musician! Choose your own path through this multiple-ending story.

♫ A Sneak Peek at ♫

No Ordinary Sound

A Melody Classic

Volume 1

Melody's adventures continue in the
first volume of her classic stories.

ig Momma brought the roast in and everyone took their places around the table, with Poppa at one end and Daddy at the other. With Yvonne home from college, the family was truly all together, the way their Sundays used to be.

"Did you study all the time, Vonnie?" Melody asked. Mommy had gone to college at Tuskegee, and this year Dwayne had applied and been accepted. Melody knew that her parents hoped all their children would graduate from Tuskegee one day, too.

Yvonne shook her head so that her small earrings sparkled. "There's so much more to do at school besides studying," she said, reaching for more gravy.

"Like what?" Poppa asked, propping his elbows on the table. Melody held back a giggle when she saw Big Momma frown the same way Mommy had, but Poppa paid no attention.

"Well, last week before finals a bunch of us went out to help black people in the community register to vote," Yvonne said. "And do you know, a lady told me she was too afraid to sign up."

"Why was she afraid?" Melody interrupted.

"Because somebody threw a rock through her next-door neighbor's window after her neighbor voted," Yvonne explained, her eyes flashing with anger. "This is 1963! How can anybody get away with that?"

Melody looked from Yvonne to her father. "You always say not voting is like not being able to talk. Why wouldn't anybody want to talk?"

Daddy sighed. "It's not that she doesn't want to vote, Melody. There are a lot of unfair rules down South that keep our people from exercising their rights. Some white people will do anything, including scaring black people, to keep change from happening. They don't want to share jobs or neighborhoods or schools with us. Voting is like a man or woman's voice speaking out to change those laws and rules."

"And it's not just about voting," Mommy said. "Remember what Rosa Parks did in Montgomery? She stood up for her rights."

"You mean she *sat down* for her rights," Melody said. Melody knew all about Mrs. Parks, who got arrested for simply sitting down on a city bus. She had paid her fare like everybody else, but because she

was a Negro the bus driver told her she had to give her seat to a white person! *But that happened eight years ago,* Melody realized. *Why haven't things changed?*

"Aren't we just as good as anybody else?" Melody asked as she looked around the table. "The laws should be fair everywhere, for everybody, right?"

"That's not always the way life works," Poppa said.

"Why not?" Lila asked.

Poppa sat back and rubbed his silvery mustache. That always meant he was about to tell a story.

"Back in Alabama, there was a white farmer who owned the land next to ours. Palmer was his name. Decent fellow. We went into town the same day to sell our peanut crops. It wasn't a good growing year, but I'd lucked out with twice as many sacks of peanuts as Palmer. Well, at the market they counted and weighed his sacks. Then they counted and weighed my sacks. Somehow Palmer got twice as much money as I got for selling half the crop I had. They never even checked the quality of what we had, either."

"What?" Lila blurted out.

"How?" Melody scooted to the edge of her chair.

"Wait, now." Poppa waved his grandchildren

quiet. "I asked the man to weigh it again, but he refused. I complained. Even Palmer spoke up for me. But that man turned to me and said, 'Boy—'"

"He called you *boy*?" Dwayne interrupted, putting his fork down.

"'Boy,'" Poppa continued, "'this is all you're gonna get. And if you keep up this trouble, you won't have any farm to go back to!'"

Melody's mouth fell open. "What was he talking about? You did have a farm," she said, glancing at Big Momma.

"He meant we were in danger of losing our farm— our home—because your grandfather spoke out to a white man," Big Momma explained. She shook her head slowly. "As hard as we'd worked to buy that land, as hard as it was for colored people to own any-thing in Alabama, we decided that day that we had to sell and move north."

Although Melody had heard many of her grand-father's stories about life in Alabama before, she'd never heard this one. And as she considered it, she realized that on their many trips down South, she'd never seen the old family farm. Maybe her

grandparents didn't want to go back.

Melody sighed. Maybe the lady Yvonne mentioned didn't want to risk losing *her* home if she "spoke out" by voting. But Yvonne was right—it was hard to understand how that could happen in the United States of America in 1963!

Poppa was shaking his head. "It's a shame that colored people today still have to be afraid of standing up or speaking out for themselves."

"Negroes," Mommy corrected him.

"Black people," Yvonne said firmly.

"Well, what *are* we supposed to call ourselves?" Lila asked.

Melody thought about how her grandparents usually said "colored." They were older and from the South, and Big Momma said that's what was proper when they were growing up. Mommy and Daddy mostly said "Negroes." But ever since she went to college, Yvonne was saying "black people." Melody noticed that Mommy and Daddy were saying it sometimes, too. She liked the way it went with "white people," like a matched set. But sometimes she wished they didn't need all these color words at all. Melody

spoke up. "What about 'Americans'?" she said.

Yvonne still seemed upset. "That's right, Dee-Dee. We're Americans. We have the same rights as white Americans. There shouldn't be any separate water fountains or waiting rooms or public bathrooms. Black Americans deserve equal treatment and equal pay. And sometimes we have to remind people."

"How do we remind them?" Lila asked. Melody was wondering the same thing.

"By not shopping at stores that won't hire black workers," Yvonne explained. "By picketing in front of a restaurant that won't serve black people. By marching."

"You won't catch me protesting or picketing or marching in any street," Dwayne interrupted, working on his third helping of potatoes. "I'm gonna be onstage or in the recording studio, making music and getting famous."

Mr. Ellison shook his head, and Melody knew there was going to be another argument, the way there always was when Dwayne talked about becoming a music star.

About the Author

ERIN FALLIGANT grew up in the seventies, ten years after Melody's stories take place. But like Melody, she loved singing into her hairbrush to music from Motown star Diana Ross. Erin had a passion for writing stories—and dreamed of becoming an author one day. Now she has written more than 25 books for children, including advice books, picture books, and contemporary fiction. Erin writes from her home in Madison, Wisconsin, and often takes breaks to cuddle with a cat or to turn up the music and dance.

About the Author

DENISE LEWIS PATRICK grew up in
the town of Natchitoches, Louisiana. Lots
of relatives lived nearby, so there was
always someone watching out for her and
always someone to play with. Every week,
Denise and her brother went to the library,
where she would read and dream in the
children's room overlooking a wonderful
river. She wrote and illustrated her first
book when she was ten. Today, Denise lives
in New Jersey, but she loves returning to
her hometown and taking her four sons to
all the places she enjoyed as a child.

Advisory Board

*American Girl extends its deepest appreciation
to the advisory board that authenticated Melody's stories.*

Julian Bond
Chairman Emeritus, NAACP Board of Directors, and founding
member of Student Nonviolent Coordinating Committee (SNCC)

Rebecca de Schweinitz
Associate Professor of History, Brigham Young University,
and author of *If We Could Change the World: Young People and
America's Long Struggle for Racial Equality* (Chapel Hill:
University of North Carolina Press, 2009)

Gloria House
Director and Professor Emerita, African and African American
Studies, University of Michigan–Dearborn, and SNCC Field
Secretary, Lowndes County, Alabama, 1963-1965

Juanita Moore
President and CEO of Charles H. Wright Museum of
African American History, Detroit, and founding executive director
of the National Civil Rights Museum, Memphis, Tennessee

Thomas J. Sugrue
Professor of History, New York University, and author of
*Sweet Land of Liberty: The Forgotten Struggle for Civil Rights
in the North* (Random House, 2008)

JoAnn Watson
Native of Detroit, ordained minister, and former
executive director of the Detroit NAACP